JAMIE AND THE
LITTLE PEOPLE

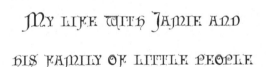

MY LIFE WITH JAMIE AND
HIS FAMILY OF LITTLE PEOPLE

Wayne E. Lofton

ISBN: 1492119644
ISBN-13: 9781492119647
Library of Congress Control Number: 2013915550
CreateSpace Independent Publishing Platform
North Charleston, South Carolina

PRELUDE

To my readers

Some of you are going to
believe this story, and some
are not.
For those of you that doubt,
I'm sure that you will wish
you could believe that it was all true
by the time you finish the story.
Just remember all the unexplained
things that have happened in your
past, like whisperings of which you could
not find the source, or movements seen
out of the corner of your eye, just to name
a few.
Hmm, could it possibly be?

CHAPTER I

It was just getting daylight, around seven in the morning, when I took off from the house with the dogs. I would usually take them for a walk at about this time when I was home and it was not pouring down rain.

We—my wife, Linda, and I—lived on a dead-end road, and it made a good place to walk Bruno and Mercy. Bruno is a big dog, half golden retriever and half airedale—we think, anyway. He weighs around one hundred and twenty pounds. Mercy is half golden retriever and half Maltese; she weighs about eighty pounds, so she is not little either. We walked a half mile in one direction and then headed home, twice a day. It was good exercise for the dogs, and for us too. Many times, Linda couldn't go because she had to be at work early, which was the case this day.

We would see lots of different kinds of birds and animals on our walks. It was not uncommon to see deer, coyotes, coons, ducks, geese, and sometimes nutria, which are big, rat-like animals almost the size of beaver. Bruno hated the nutria; he tried to kill every one he saw. He would get pretty chewed up sometimes. They have razor-sharp teeth and know how to use them.

Anyway, this was a pretty nice day, not raining, and the wind was calm. There were broken clouds, so I could see the sun coming up. We had been walking for about five minutes. Bruno was out front, wanting to take off, and Mercy was lollygagging around behind me as usual. We had almost got to the culvert where a small creek runs under and then parallels the road for about fifty yards.

This creek is where we usually saw the nutria, coons, and ducks. It runs into the Santiam River during the winter, when we have lots of water, but it dries up in the heat of the summer. It was probably about half full on this day.

All of a sudden, Bruno yipped and ran for the culvert. Mercy heard him and followed. They stopped right where the culvert comes out from under the road. They were standing dead still, not barking or moving, although Bruno's tail was wagging a little bit. Now, this was very unusual; I had never seen either dog act this way. They were pointed toward the end of the culvert, at something under the brush. The blackberries grow over it, concealing it from view, and I couldn't tell what they were looking at.

One thing for sure: they weren't mad or scared.

I finally walked right over beside them, got down on my knees, and peered under the brush. My God, I just about fell over. I think Bruno licked my cheek just about the same time it dawned on me what I was looking at, and that didn't help matters at all.

Now, I've always considered myself to be a pretty level-headed, outdoorsy kind of a person. I spent four years in the armed service, twenty years wearing a badge as a game officer, and twenty years as a fishing guide. I've never seen anything in the outdoors that I couldn't logically explain or identify.

But what I was looking at right then just threw all my logic right out the window.

I know you are not going to believe this—I didn't—but here it goes anyway.

On the end of that culvert sat a little old man about two feet tall. He looked just like a full-grown person, but smaller—a lot smaller. You could tell he wasn't a child by his wrinkles. Good Lord, he kinda looked like one of the dwarfs in the *Snow White* movie, except this wasn't a cartoon character. He was real and alive. He had a brown coat on over green pants, a red hat that was pointed on the end, and little brown boots that were also pointed.

The little man didn't see or hear me or the dogs; the water was making too much noise, and he was too intent on what he was doing. He was...you're not going to believe this...fishing with a little pole and bobber off of the end of that culvert.

Now, I have high blood pressure, and I take a pre-scribed half pill every morning for it and try to keep my pulse rate down. While I was lying there—oh yes, I was flat on my stomach by that time—I wished I had taken a whole pill that morning because I could feel my heart beating fast in my chest, very fast.

I watched him for about ten minutes, and by the end of that time, I had calmed down considerably. He was actually catching fish. They looked like little chubs or squaw fish to me, only three or four inches long, but they were really giving him a tussle. You have to think about it for a minute: he wasn't very big, and neither was his fishing pole. A four-inch fish to him was like a twenty-pound salmon to us. I might add, he was no novice at what he was doing either; he could handle that pole quite efficiently.

I noticed the hooks that he was using looked familiar, and then it dawned on me. Last summer, I had been getting some trout gear ready to go to the upper lakes. I'd left a box of size fourteen single-egg hooks out on my workbench, but the next morning, I couldn't find them. I figured I had just misplaced them and never thought much more about it until now. I looked at what he was using for bait, which was little pieces of worms, and noticed he was putting them on a little gold hook that appeared to be about a size fourteen. Everything he had on and that he was using looked kinda homemade, but those little gold hooks didn't. Those were store-bought. A light bulb went off. My gosh, I had been missing quite a few little things since we'd moved to our present house three years ago. I hadn't thought much about it before. I am getting older and always figured that was the reason.

He had put the fish he'd caught on a piece of string and hung them in the water. He had five or six fish on the string and was putting another on when he reached down with his other hand, picked up his pole, and then did the most amazing thing. He looked up at me and the dogs, grinned great big, and just vanished—fish, fishing pole, and all. Now what I mean by "vanished" is that he moved so fast that if I had blinked, I wouldn't have seen him move at all. I saw the brush moving. That is how I saw he had left.

Good Lord, I was flabbergasted. I stayed there for a few seconds longer just to collect my thoughts, and then I jumped up and followed the dogs that were going on down the road.

I didn't know what to do. I didn't dare tell anyone; no one would believe me anyway. I wasn't sure I believed it myself. *Gosh,* I just realized, *if someone did believe me, there would be people all over my place and the surrounding fields looking for that little man, and I surely don't want that.* OK, I decided not to tell anyone. Well, maybe Linda, but that was all.

We had walked almost to the spot where we usually turn around when something else dawned on me. That little man had been smoking a pipe when I first saw him. He had laid it down on the culvert while he landed the fish. I never saw him pick it up when he left. I turned around and ran all the way back to the culvert.

I got down on my stomach again and looked under the brush at the end of the culvert. I couldn't see anything, so I wiggled my way down almost to the culvert—and then I spotted it. It was a little pipe made out of a tree limb, and it was still warm. I couldn't see anything else, so I started crawling my way back out of there and prayed that one of my neighbors didn't come along and see me. My God, they would think that I was crazy.

Hmm, if they heard what I had seen, they would *know* I was.

I got back up on the road, stuck that little pipe in my pocket, and took off for home. That little pipe was the only thing I had to prove my sanity, at least to myself, and I made sure to keep it safe.

Linda got home from work late that night, and I didn't say anything until we went to bed and turned out the lights. I told her what had happened, except I didn't tell her about the pipe.

I finished the story, and she didn't say anything for about five seconds. Then she just burst out laughing. I thought she was going to fall out of bed. When she finished her hysterical onslaught, she said, and I quote, "My God, honey, you are home too much! You need a life." And then she laughed some more.

I told her good night.

CHAPTER 2

Linda never would believe me. I even took the little pipe out of my drawer, where I had been hiding it, and showed it to her. All she said was, "That's a cute little pipe. How long did it take you to make it?" Oh yes, and then she laughed some more. I told her that one of these days, she might wake up and find that little man standing on the end of the bed. She said that if that happened, it would probably be the end of the little man. I might add that she didn't laugh then. So I decided not to mention the incident to her anymore for a while.

I did mention to my son and my mother what had happened. My son thought it was cool but looked at me funny out of the corner of his eyes. He nodded his head affirmatively and agreed with everything I said. My mother, on the other hand, thought I was losing it and even said to my son and Linda that she thought I needed some help.

I fibbed a little bit, trying to get somebody to believe me. I tore a corner off of a piece of paper that was on the kitchen counter one morning, wrote the word "pipe" on it, and then took it with Linda and me on our walk with the pooches. When I got to the culvert, I reached down, acted like I had picked up the piece of paper, and said, "Hmm, what is this?"

Linda said, "Give it to me, I want to see it." So I did. She looked at it, smiled, looked up at me, and said, "Good grief!" I did my best to carry it through, but I didn't do very well. To make matters worse, when we got back to the house, she found the piece of paper that I had torn the corner off and brought it to me with a grin. Lord, she is a better cop than I was. You'd think I would have thrown that piece of paper in the garbage, but no, I left it right out in plain sight. That cinched it. Now she would never believe me.

OK, no more telling anybody about the little man. I knew nobody would believe me. In fact, I was starting to doubt myself. Boy, if dogs could talk...Bruno and Mercy were there, they saw him. One day when I was outside playing with them, I knelt down, put my arms around Bruno's neck, and said, "Well, buddy, it's just you and me against the world. Nobody else believes us."

I kept looking for the little guy or any sign of him for weeks but never found anything. Every time the dogs barked, I'd jump up and run to look. I looked for tracks in the dirt and mud. I was going to put pieces of food out around the house and property, but I figured the birds and little animals would eat them. Besides, he didn't look underfed to me anyway. I was going to put the pipe

JAMIE and The LITTLE PEOPLE

back where I'd found it but decided against it, mainly because that was the only thing I could use to actually prove to myself that I had seen what I had.

I would sit back and think of the time I did see him and try to remember everything about him. I had actually had quite some time to watch him while he was fishing. Everything he had on looked homemade. I remember seeing stitching on the side of his pants and coat. The colors of his clothes seemed faded—or at least, they weren't as bright as the clothes we wear. In fact, for a better word, he looked kinda woodsy.

Then one day it happened—or I thought it happened. I was out behind the barn picking up limbs that had blown out of the trees in the last storm. Some geese were flying over, and I stopped what I was doing and looked up to watch them. When they got over a big oak tree that was about a hundred feet from me, I noticed something on a limb about twenty feet up. I was kinda looking into the sun and couldn't see it real clear, but it didn't look like a bird or a squirrel. I shaded my eyes with my hands to see better, and it moved behind the tree on the limb. I dropped the branch I was holding, opened the gates, and ran over to the oak. I had to get through a little brush to get right under it, but when I did, there was nothing there. I looked all over. There was no big bird flying away, no animal up the tree, absolutely nothing around that I could see. I was a little bit upset, to say the least.

Actually, I had put the little man incident to the back of my mind by the time this happened. Not to say that I had forgotten him, just that I had more important things to think about. I cannot honestly say what was up that tree watching me, but it made me wonder. And if it was the little man, what the dickens was he doing up that tree, and how did he get there? There are very few limbs at the bottom of an oak tree.

CHAPTER 3

Time went by, and I got back to my old self. My blood pressure went back down, and I wasn't near as nervous anymore, jumping at any little noise. I got back in my same old routine of walking the dogs every morning and evening and working around the place all day. The only time I would actually think about the little man was when I saw the pipe in my drawer along with my nail clippers, pencils, pens, and other articles. I thought about putting the pipe in a frame and hanging it on the wall, but I decided against it. For one thing, someday I might have to give it back. And another thing: I'm sure Linda wouldn't be greatly pleased. In fact, there would be better words to describe her displeasure, but I won't use them.

One morning about three months after I had first seen the little man, I was walking the dogs as usual when I stopped along the creek. The dogs had been barking, and I heard some splashing, so I thought there was some critter in the water. The sun was out, it was a nice day, and I could see almost to the bottom. All of a sudden, a fish jumped clear out of the water, right in front of me. It was about six or seven inches long, and I think it was a trout, but I'm not sure. What really got me was that there was a piece of fishing line hanging out of its mouth. I must have stood there for ten seconds with my mouth hanging down to my knees before I realized what had happened. Somebody had been fishing there not long before I arrived with the dogs and had broken the line off in the fish. I had seen no one around, no cars, tracks, or anything. Besides, I had never seen anyone fishing in that creek except the little man; in fact, I think it is closed to fishing by law.

OK, that left only one explanation. That fish had been hooked and lost by a very small person who couldn't be seen from the road. Needless to say, I got a little excited and started looking all over the place, but I never found anything. I went back home and never said a word about it to Linda or anyone else.

Not long after the fish incident, I was running the tractor behind the barn and had shut it off to work on a post with a shovel. I heard some buzzing—or what sounded like buzzing. At first I thought it was bees, but then I thought it couldn't be. It was too early in the year and too cold for bees to be making that much noise. I decided to go see what it was. The noise seemed to be coming from some brush, and as I got closer, it got louder and didn't sound like buzzing anymore, but little squeaky voices. Now, I know this sounds stupid, but I don't know how better to explain it, except maybe—remember the little talking mice in the Disney movies? It kinda sounded like them. Anyway, as I got closer, the noise stopped, and of course I never found anything or heard any more. I stayed in that brush all morning. The more I thought about it, the surer I was that I'd heard little voices, but I couldn't tell what they said. In fact, I don't think it was English.

More frustration. I think after that, my blood pressure went back up. Let's see now, I had been seeing things that weren't there, then I started to hear little voices...wow, I knew I was losing it. Boy, if Linda knew what I wanted to tell her...never mind. You can guess what would have happened.

CHAPTER 4

One day when I went to the mailbox on the road near our driveway, I heard a funny noise from across the road. Now, this area is nothing but brush and oak trees, about four acres of them anyway, and surrounded by a large field. I couldn't see anything from where I was at, so I walked around and looked in from the field side. I still couldn't see anything, so I stooped down and walked into the brush.

I had been snooping around in there for about five minutes and was getting ready to leave when I looked down by my feet and noticed a dead bird. I had almost stepped on it because it was brown and blended into the leaves. It was a small bird, probably a sparrow. It wasn't ruffled up like it would be if an animal had killed it; it was just lying there like it had dropped over dead. I bent down and looked at it closer and noticed a small stick protruding from its head, just behind its left eye. Thinking at the time that it must have flown into a tree or something, I picked it up and put it into my pocket. Now, I don't know why I did that. I'm not in the habit of picking up dead animals and putting them in my pocket.

I went to my workshop, took the little bird out of my pocket, and laid it on my bench. I took the mail to the house and forgot about the bird until later in the afternoon when I went back out to the shop. I put the bird under my shop light; it has a big magnifying glass on it. I couldn't see any injury to the bird, with the exception of the stick behind the eye.

I couldn't believe I was doing this, but I thought I had gone this far, I might as well pull out the stick. It protruded about two inches. I still figured the bird had flown into a tree or something. Anyway, I very carefully tried to pull it, but it didn't move, so I gave it a little jerk and out it came. It looked different. It was very straight and clean-looking, with the exception of the broken end protruding from the bird. Not what you would expect a small limb to look like. Maybe that was why I was so curious about it in the first place. I laid it on the bench and went to get some water to wash the blood off. I was beginning to feel like a real crime-scene investigator at about this time. I could imagine what Linda would say if she knew what I was doing. Well, I got a bottle cap full of water, found my tweezers in a drawer, and proceeded to clean off the stick.

To my astonishment, it was not a piece of a limb. It was smooth and straight and as sharp as a needle, with a barb on the end. That was why I had trouble getting it out. It was definitely man-made and looked like the business end of a small arrow or dart.

OK, that did it. I had to go sit down in a chair for a minute. I was sure my blood pressure went up; I know my pulse was racing. The noise that I'd heard must have been the bird falling out of a tree. I never heard the bow or blowgun that shot it. Besides, if it was an arrow, it was so small that its bow would have to be very small too. Probably too small to hear.

Where the little arrow had hit the bird was in a perfect place to kill it instantly. It would have dropped straight down off of where it was sitting. That gave me an idea. The other piece of the arrow had to be close to where I'd found the bird. I never noticed it because I wasn't looking for anything like that at the time. Needless to say, I went flying out of the shop and across the road.

I found the exact spot, got down on my hands and knees, and crawled around for about fifteen minutes. But I never did find anything lying on the ground. Feeling a little flustered (and my back hurt anyway), I sat down and looked up to where the bird should have been when it was shot. And then I spotted something about seven feet up, lodged in the branches of a bush. I reached over and shook the base of the bush. The end of the little arrow fell to the ground, right in front of me.

I picked it up and immediately went back to my shop. After putting the two pieces together, the arrow measured close to six inches long and was about an eighth of an inch in diameter. It had one barbed end, as I said before, and small pieces of feathers on the other end, just like a store-bought arrow. I believe they call that fletching. Also, the feathered end of the arrow was notched for a bow string, so it was in fact an arrow, not a dart.

The bird must have been shot when I was at the mailbox. Not only should I have seen the bird fall, I should have been able to see the person who shot it. Then I wondered: what if the little person was up in the tree with the bird?

OK, I figured, there were too many things happening around me that I couldn't logically explain. It was just a matter of time before I made actual contact with the little person or persons responsible. In fact, I remember that thinking of it that way made me feel a lot better. I had finally come to the conclusion that these things were really happening and not figments of my imagination. I still refrained from telling any more people about it. The reaction I had received from my wife, mother, and son was enough. In fact, I had decided not to say anything more to them about it either, at least not at that time. Maybe later, when I had more proof.

CHAPTER 5

Over the next few months, a number of things happened that I guess I would call close encounters, for lack of better words. Nothing very substantial, but an unexplained event about once a week.

And then one day, it happened. It changed my life.

I was working in the barn. It was about two in the afternoon. I was moving some machinery around and cleaning up a bit when I heard a strange noise outside. It was actually coming from behind the building. It sounded a lot like the buzzing that I had heard before, but not quite as loud. At first I didn't go outside to check on it, but then decided I would, just a lot quieter this time. I didn't take the dogs with me. As I snuck around the barn, the noise got louder. As I described before, it sounded like a little voice. It sounded like only one voice, and it sounded like someone was hurt or in distress.

The voice was coming from the other side of an old stump. I got down on my hands and knees and crawled.

The closer I got, the surer I was that it was a little human voice speaking English and crying for help. As I peered around the stump, I saw a little person sitting on the ground and holding his or her left ankle. I wasn't sure if the little person was male or female because of the long hair, but I presumed male because he was dressed like the little man I had seen months prior. The only real difference was the lack of a hat, and this little person seemed a lot smaller.

One thing for sure, the little man was in a whole lot of pain. He was crying and sobbing. He was yelling something that I couldn't understand at first because of the crying, and then I caught the word "Dad." Then it dawned on me. This was a child, and that's the reason he seemed so much smaller.

The little person didn't see me for about a minute, but when he did, wow, did he scream—at least I thought it was a scream. He produced a noise that made my ears hurt. I didn't know quite what to do, so I backed up and lay down on my stomach, meanwhile talking very calmly, or at least trying to. I know my voice was shaking as I kept saying, "I won't hurt you" and "Don't be afraid." It wasn't working; in fact, things seemed to be getting worse. There was no doubt that the little person would have been gone if not for his injured leg.

About that time, I heard a commotion behind me. Turning around, I saw Bruno jump the gate and run toward me. It was no wonder that he heard all the noise; it was loud enough. I figured that seeing me lying on the ground, he was coming to my rescue, but no, he ran right up and laid his head down on the ground by the little person. I thought, *Oh, no, that will really scare him*, but boy, was I wrong. I then witnessed the most astonishing thing: the little person leaned over and laid his head and shoulder on the top of Bruno's head. He continued to sob but had quit screaming, and Bruno didn't move a muscle. My God, I had tears running down my cheek.

The boy finally quit sobbing a little bit and tried to say something, but I couldn't understand him, so I started to move a little closer. I immediately figured out that wasn't the thing to do. His eyes got big like he was going to scream again, and Bruno growled at the same time. Now, Bruno has never growled at me in his entire life, and this made me feel a little weird—betrayed, or something. I did sit up because my stomach was getting wet from the grass.

I told him again that I wouldn't hurt him and meanwhile reached over and started petting Bruno's back. He sat up and watched me, looking back and forth from my face to Bruno's, apparently trying to decide what to do next. He then said, very slowly and very clearly, in a small, high voice, "My leg hurts, bad." I said that I was sorry and asked him what I could do to help. He grabbed his ears and said, "Don't talk so loud, please. It hurts my ears." I couldn't understand that because his screaming had really hurt *my* ears. I know I must have looked a little puzzled because he said, "What?"

I said, "Your screaming hurt my ears!"

He said, between sobs, "I wasn't screaming. I was calling Bruno." Now, that about floored me. I was beginning to wonder whose dog he was.

From that time on, I always talked to little people in a slow, soft voice, almost a whisper. I asked the little boy what his name was and how old he was. He told me, still sobbing, that his name was Davey, and he was twelve years old. I asked him if I could look at his leg. He was very hesitant at first, then agreed to let me, but I noticed he reached over and grabbed a handful of Bruno's fur for reassurance.

Now, let me say right now that this little guy looked just like any other twelve-year-old boy, just a lot smaller. He was probably around a foot and a half tall, but other than that, perfectly proportioned. His clothes were similar to those of the first little person that I had seen, but in different colors, and he didn't have a hat on. He did have a band around his head, probably to hold his hair out of his eyes.

I started to look at his injured leg as I asked how he had hurt himself, trying to keep his mind off of what I was doing. It was his right ankle. He had some little boots on, but they came off easy. He didn't have any socks, thank goodness, so as I held his leg in my left hand, I could see it plainly. I didn't think it was broken. There was a little discoloration already, but I didn't notice any deformity. It seemed to be extremely painful, but sprains usually are. I didn't know quite what to do. I didn't dare give him an aspirin or any other pill. He was so small, I wouldn't know how much to give him. Besides, he might have a reaction to our medicine.

While I looked at his leg, he told me that he had been up in the tree that was close to us. He said he had slipped on something and twisted his leg when he jumped to the ground. I asked him what he was doing in the tree. He looked a little embarrassed and said, "I was looking for Bruno; I come and see Bruno almost every day." That didn't really surprise me; there was no doubt that Bruno knew the little guy quite well.

I said, "You must like Bruno, huh?"

He said, "Yup, Bruno and me are buddies."

I asked, "What about Mercy, do you like her too?"

He said, "Sure, but I like Bruno more." He added, "I don't like your cat, though, he scares me. He tried to catch me one time, but I ran away."

I said, "Yes, you are pretty fast. A lot of times, I thought I saw you, but in a blink of an eye you were gone."

He laughed then, kinda. He had still been sobbing a bit while talking. He said, "Nothing sees us unless we want them to. We can run too fast." Then he started crying a little and added, "Unless we get hurt and can't run. And then anything can see us, and get us too." He said, "The big birds are the worst. They are very dangerous, and they try to get us all the time."

I said, "I thought I heard you calling for your dad or something when I first found you."

"You did," he said. "I needed help before a big bird saw me."

"Well, he must not have been able to hear you; maybe he was too far away."

He said, "No, he wasn't. He heard me," and gave me a funny look.

I asked why he didn't come.

He paused, still giving me a funny look, and said, "He did. He is right behind you."

I was still sitting down, holding Davey's leg. I slowly looked back over my left shoulder and caught my breath at what I saw. There were five little people standing behind me. Apparently they had been there for some time, watching. Four of them had bows in their hands, with arrows, but the bows weren't drawn back. I could tell they were all grown-ups, all about the same size as the first little person I had seen. They didn't look mad or mean or anything, but on the other hand, they weren't smiling either. It gave me kind of a queer feeling. I didn't know what to say or do.

The one not carrying a bow started to walk around me. That one didn't have a hat on and looked different than the other four. Then, understanding, I knew why: it was a female. In fact, she was beautiful, in a small way. She was slighter built than the rest but almost as tall. Like I said, she didn't have a hat on, but she had a band around her head, like the boy. She did have pants, boots, and a coat on, like the rest of them. While she was walking around me, she looked into my face the whole time. She walked right up to me and the boy and looked down to see what I was doing. I looked up at the boy's face and noticed that he had quit sobbing and was looking at me with a smile. He said, "This is my mom."

I could see the resemblance. They both had the same color hair, a light brown, and their facial features were a lot the same. She was taller than he was, of course, and had a feminine look about her.

She bent down and took Davey's leg out of my hand very gently and inspected it all over. She said something very quietly that I could not hear. Davey said that he had slipped when he jumped out of the tree. I saw kind of a scolding look come from his mom, and Davey just looked down. I chuckled to myself and thought, *I've seen that look before, years ago, coming from my mother—and not too long ago from my wife.* I thought, *My gosh, they act and look just like people*...and then thought, *You idiot, they* are *people, just smaller.* She turned around and glanced at me as if she had understood what I was thinking. I felt a little foolish.

I asked Davey what his mother's name was. She turned to me and said, "My name is Sara. And you can talk to me, you know." That sounded a little snooty, and I thought, *Wow, women are all the same, no matter what size they are* and grinned to myself.

Just about that time, I saw a movement on my right. One of the men had walked around behind me and Bruno and came up beside Davey and stopped. He didn't look at me but was more interested in Davey. He squatted down, looking at the leg, and said, "My name is Jamie, his dad." For some reason, right then, I recognized him. He was the little person that I had first seen, the one fishing in the creek, months before. He turned to Davey and asked, "Where is your shoulder bag and your bow?" Davey told him that he had left them home; he had just wanted to see Bruno for a minute. Jamie said, "I guess maybe from now on you will keep them with you. What if a big bird had got to you before Bruno and Wayne?"

Davey looked down and said, "I'm sorry, Dad."

I immediately asked, "How did you know my name?"

He looked at me and grinned, and then said, "I've known your name for a long time. All of us have."

CHAPTER 6

I really wanted to ask Jamie a lot of questions, but I didn't feel like right then was the time to be doing it. His son was hurt, and you could see that it truly bothered him. Also, there were a lot of other people present, including his wife, and she didn't appear to be in a very good mood either.

My attention turned to her and what she was doing. She opened her shoulder bag, one of which they all seemed to be carrying, took out a small package, and unfolded its paper. Inside the paper was a light golden, glowing substance. She began applying some of the stuff to Dave's injured leg. When she was done, she put the package away and took something else out of her bag, gave it to Davey, and told him to chew it. She turned to Jamie and said, "He'll be all right in a short time." She turned away, then turned back to Jamie and said, "This is really your fault, you know." Jamie's cheeks turned red above his beard, and he looked down. I thought, *Hmmm, I have been in that position before, myself.*

Almost immediately, I could see that Davey wasn't in pain anymore. He didn't appear to be drugged; it was just that his leg wasn't hurting. Also, the gold-colored, salve-like stuff on Davey's leg seemed to be disappearing. After two or three minutes, it was totally gone, and Davey stood up. Now, just ask me if I was impressed or what. I wanted to ask what Sara had put on him but thought better of it. I don't think she was in the frame of mind to answer any questions from me.

Sara stood up and told Davey she would see him at home. She looked at her husband, then looked at me, and then just vanished in kind of a blur. It startled me. I jerked back and said, "Good grief."

Jamie and his son both looked at me and grinned. Then I noticed that the other men had left too. I never saw them leave, but they must have left about the time Davey stood up.

I guess they thought he didn't need any more protection.

Jamie told Davey to go on home and that he would be coming along shortly. Davey looked at me and said thank you, reached down and rubbed Bruno on his head, and left in a blur, just like his mother had. I didn't jump this time. Jamie reached down and started petting Bruno. He said to me, "I guess I owe you a lot of explanations, huh?"

I said, "Well, I do have a few questions." I didn't tell him that he and all his little friends and family had just about driven me crazy during the previous few months.

He said, "Very few people of your size know about us, and the ones who do usually keep it to themselves like you have." I thought, *Boy, if you only knew what I told my wife and family*. He said, "I'm sure you told your wife. And she probably didn't believe you."

I laughed and said, "You are very right."

He smiled. "You know you owe me a pipe. That was one of the best pipes I've ever had."

"Did you make it?" He answered no, and that they had pipe makers who did only that. I told him I would give his pipe back anytime he wanted it, and he replied that there wasn't any hurry; he had plenty of others. Meanwhile, he took one out of his pocket and lit it.

When I first saw Jamie fishing at the culvert, I had thought he was old and fat. I made a mistake. The little man I was looking at right then wasn't old, and he wasn't fat either. In fact, he didn't look fat at all; he looked really strong. He did have a white beard, though; maybe that's why I thought he was old at first. I wondered how heavy he was, so I tried to think of some way to ask without insulting him. So I said, "Gosh, you move so fast for being so strongly built." He looked at me for a second and then just started laughing. I felt like an idiot.

He said, "That's OK. I know some of us look a little fat. In fact, some of us are fat, but we aren't near as heavy as we look. I will show you. Hold your arm straight out." I did, and he placed his arms over it and lifted his feet off the ground. Good grief, I hardly felt any weight at all. I swear, he couldn't have weighed more than five pounds. I asked how that could be possible, and he said that he wasn't sure, but it had something to do with the way they were built. Their bones were more like a bird's instead of heavy like those of other animals, and that was one of the reasons they could move so fast when they wanted to. He said there were some other reasons, but he had better not tell me because if the elders found out, he would get in trouble. Boy, that got my curiosity up.

I asked him if he had any other children, and he replied, "Yes, two girls."

"Where do all of you live?"

He looked at me for a second and said, "If you mean me and my family, we live right over there in the woods," and pointed to the timber across the field. He added, "There are eight other families that live in the same woods."

My mouth about fell open on that one, so I said, "My gosh, how many little people are there?" He said that he really had no idea, adding that there were probably thirty or forty families that lived on this side of the big river and that he had never been on the other side, although he had heard of some families that lived on the other side too.

I asked him why his wife had said that Davey's injury was his fault. He said that Davey had got really fond of Bruno and came over here to see him all the time. He said that he had planned for me to catch him fishing just to see how I would react because he knew that I would catch Davey sometime, hanging around our place. He said that he probably should have put a stop to Davey's visits—Sara, anyway, thought he should have.

Jamie stood up and said, "Wayne, I know you have a lot of questions, but I'm sure that there will be plenty of time in the future to answer them." He said that he should be getting back so Sara didn't get angrier and that he was going to hear a lot of told-you-so's as it was. He was grinning when he added that he could handle it, though, and he started to laugh when he said, "Wives can get a little testy sometimes, huh?" He was still laughing when he said, "Don't we love them though?" and with that, there was kind of a whoosh, and he was gone.

I could hear him laugh as he went away. It kinda sounded like a bumble bee when it flies away.

Bruno, who had been lying there all this time, finally sat up and looked at me with his tongue hanging out, panting. He looked like he was grinning. I told him that he was a traitor. He still looked like he was grinning. I got up and proceeded to the house, letting Bruno back through the gate. I wondered how that big dog could get over that five-foot gate, but I had enough things to think about for the day. Bruno and that gate were at the bottom of the list.

I went into the house, made myself a cup of tea, and sat down to think. Linda wasn't home, she was working—which was probably a good thing; otherwise, I would have probably blurted out to her everything that had happened that day. And after thinking about it, I realized that it might have been a big mistake. I was tired of her and the rest of my family thinking I was losing it. One day in the future, I was sure, I would get the chance to introduce Jamie and his family to Linda, and on that day, boy, would it be funny or what. In fact, just thinking about it made me laugh and spill my tea.

I got to thinking about everything Jamie had told me. I wondered about how many others knew about the little people. My gosh, I was sixty years old, and I had never seen or heard about them before. Yes, I had read fairy tales and stories about elves and things, but no real factual or upfront encounters like I just had. Maybe those who had seen them acted like I had and really didn't believe it. Or they wouldn't tell anyone because they didn't want to be labeled idiots. Oh well, I had heard enough stories about UFOs, monsters in lakes, the Devil's Triangle, sasquatches, and things like that (I might add that I never believed them), and here was a real-life phenomenon living right under everyone's nose, and very few—if any, other than me—knew about it.

Prior to that day, I must admit (and I've said it before), I was feeling a little foolish. The family members who I had confided in thought maybe that I was veering off the straight and narrow, but after what happened that day, I was feeling pretty special. I didn't have a big urge to tell anyone about the little people anymore; in fact, I felt a little protective. Maybe there were others who had had my experience and felt the same way. I just couldn't believe that they had been around for so long and no one else knew about them.

And another thing: I had thought they were a little backward and woodsy, but now I had a suspicion that they had knowledge that was more advanced than ours. For instance, the medicine that Sara gave Davey. Wow, I had never seen anything like that before. The stuff she gave him to chew that looked like shredded bark,

I'm not sure what it was—although he did calm down considerably. The gold, powderlike substance that she put on his leg, now, I saw it work. In a matter of minutes, the swelling and discoloration were not only gone, but he stood up on his leg as if nothing had happened in the first place. If our medical community has something like that, I'm sure not aware of it. But if we had a healing substance that could apparently heal injuries like that (and God knows what else) upon contact, do you think they would let it out? I think not. My gosh, there must be countless people—millions—in this world who derive their livelihoods from some segment of the medical community. I couldn't imagine what effect an all-healing substance would have on them. Wow. After thinking about it, I saw that was another good reason to keep my mouth shut.

After all that had happened that day and all the things that I had seen, I felt that I had more questions in my mind than I did answers. In fact, I had started to feel like the keeper of a big secret. It wasn't a pleasant feeling, but I might add, it sure was an awful powerful one.

CHAPTER 7

About a week later, I was taking the dogs on their afternoon walk. It was a beautiful day, and I had left the road, walking around the big field behind the house. The dogs were way out ahead; I was walking along the edge looking for animal tracks when I saw something move into the brush about twenty feet in front of me. Thinking it was a squirrel or some other little animal, I went over, got down on my hands and knees, and stuck my head under a dead limb to take a look.

All of a sudden, there was a little voice in my left ear, asking, "What are you looking for, Wayne?" Good grief. I jerked up, bonked my head on the limb, said a bad word, and then stood up, still muttering some other bad words. I looked to my left, and there was Sara with a hand over her mouth, laughing extremely hard—too hard—and there was another little person standing beside her, not as big as Sara but looking just like her, with eyes great big, as if in shock. Sara was acting like my distress and agony were the funniest things she had ever seen.

I personally did not think it was so humorous, but after a few seconds, the pain started to diminish and I quit rubbing my head. Sara's laughing wasn't like ours; it sounded like a cross between a laugh and a little bell. It sounded really cute. Well, it would have probably sounded cuter if it hadn't been aimed at me.

I said, "You kinda startled me."

Still laughing, she said, "Well, that's apparent. Sit down."

"What?"

"Sit down on the ground and I'll take a look at your head."

I said, "It's OK," and she quit laughing and said sit down. I sat down and thought, my God, she is bossy, just like some other female I know. I almost said something but thought better of it. I sure did wish Jamie would show up though.

She walked around behind me and was apparently looking at my head because I could feel her moving my hair around. Then, I could feel her touching where I had hit it. It got cool at first and then warm, and then there was no pain at all. I put my hand up to touch the spot and got it slapped. She said to leave it alone for a little while. And then added, "Why can't men keep their dirty hands off of things?" She said the last part quietly, but I still heard it. I thought, *Boy, this meeting isn't going too well.* I could tell she was used to giving orders, and I could also tell that she was used to being obeyed. I was feeling a little sorry for Jamie.

I noticed the other little person was staring at me. I asked, "What's your name?" She wouldn't answer me, just continued looking.

Sara said, "Betsy, go ahead and answer him, it's all right. Just talk slow so he can understand you."

The girl said very slowly, "My name is Betsy..." and continued to stare at me. I reached out to shake her hand, and she disappeared in a blur. It startled me, and thinking, *Darn, I scared her*, I looked over at Sara, who was putting something away in her shoulder bag.

She said, "That was real good. What were you trying to do, anyway?" I said I was just going to shake her hand and that I was sorry, I didn't mean to scare her. Sara said that it was OK, that Betsy was eleven years old and going through that shy, timid stage. And, she had never been that close to a big person before, let alone touch one. Sara added, "Now that I think about it, you are the first big person that *I've* touched."

I said, "Well, I don't think we are that different, just in size is all."

She said kind of quietly, "That's what you think."

I looked across the field, and I couldn't see the dogs. I told Sara that I had better go get the dogs; Lord knows what they were getting into. She said that they were probably at one of their homes, most likely at hers, seeing Davey. I looked over at her and she said, "No, I don't think you can get there unless you get down on hands and knees and crawl for about thirty feet."

I was still sitting down. About that time, she dove under my arms, right next to my chest. She did it real fast, and I almost jumped up—but at about the same time, I felt a rush of air go over my head. I looked up and saw a bald eagle flying away. My gosh, that bird must have been right on top of me. It was almost out of sight, over the trees, when I looked down at Sara. She was curled up, clinging to my chest. She looked up at me and asked if it was gone. I answered yes, then added, "I thought you were just getting personal or something." She jumped back away from me, started to get red in the face, said a dirty word, I think, and vanished. I just sat there and laughed, and then thought, *I shouldn't have said that*. If I know anything about women, I know they will get even. Heck, I figured she would probably shoot me in the fanny with a little arrow or something.

I got up and was brushing myself off when I saw the dogs coming toward me. They weren't running but just walking fast, and I could see something on Bruno's back. As they got closer, I could see that it was a little person lying down, trying to hold on to Bruno's fur with both hands. When they got almost to me, the little person fell off right on his seat. It was Davey, and he was laughing so hard that he had tears. He said that he wouldn't have fallen off if he hadn't been laughing, that Bruno's fur tickles his face. I asked him if he does that very often, and he said no, at least not when his mother is around; she gets mad. He said, "By the way, Mom was sure mad a minute ago when she came home. She went stomping through the front door muttering something about big people. I knew she was with you because Betsy had come home earlier and told me so. She said she was putting medicine on a bump on your head. I thought I had better find you; Mom can be a little mean sometimes when she gets upset."

I said, "Now Davey, what could your mother possibly do to me? I'm probably four or five times her size."

He looked up at me, real quiet for a second, and then started laughing again. He said, "Wayne, I don't think you want to find out. In the first place, she is the head person of our clan. She makes the decisions for our village, her and the council of elders. Also, she is what you would call a doctor. We call her a healer, but it is more than that. She not only heals the pain of our bodies, but pain of our minds or spirits, or something like that. You will have to ask my dad to explain it to you. I don't know that much about it.

"But I do know one thing," he continued. "My mother is real powerful. She can make some very bad things happen as well as good things. About two years ago, there was a car parked in this very field, real late at night. We could hear a big-person girl screaming clear over to our house. Dad grabbed his bow and Mother grabbed her mouth tube and they left. They weren't gone very long when he heard the car start and make a lot of noise trying to get out of the field."

Davey said that that night, he could hear a man screaming as the car went fast down the road. He said that when Jamie and Sara got home, they wouldn't tell Davey and his sisters what all had happened. He said that his dad was laughing so hard, he couldn't talk, and his mother kept saying, "Well, it served him right, the idiot," and she was grinning too.

"But I think more at Dad laughing so hard than at anything else." Davey said all that his mother and father would say was that there was a man hurting a girl in the car and the window was down, that was why her screaming sounded so loud. "The man had his pants off, and Mother shot a dart from her mouth tube into the man's thing. He said the man really screamed a lot because Mother put a burning potion on the end of the dart." He also said his mother told his father that the man wouldn't be hurting any more girls with that thing for a long time. Davey had heard his father ask his mother how she had hit what she aimed at because it was so dark, and his mother answered, how could she have missed anything that big? That's when his dad started laughing hard again, until his mother told him to shut up or nobody was going to get any sleep that night.

Davey left after telling that story, and I took the dogs and headed home. I was thinking that maybe I would be nicer to Sara, or at least try not to make her mad. Also, I had a habit of relieving myself anywhere on our property when the urge hit me and no one else was around—or at least, I *thought* no one else was around. I thought maybe that was going to come to a screeching halt. Good grief, I was getting shivers up my back and other places, just thinking about the story Davey had told me.

CHAPTER 8

About a week later, I was out in the field putting poison in mole tunnels. I had been having a lot of problems with the moles. I hated to use poison, but I had tried everything else, and nothing seemed to work. I did catch a few with traps, but very few, and my field was getting to look like the surface of the moon—well, let's say, like pictures of it. No matter. Anyway, I think half of the moles in the Willamette Valley were living in my field, so I finally resigned myself to this method to reduce their population, and it seemed to be working. At least I thought it was. There seemed to be fewer molehills than when I started.

I was on my knees, bent over digging out a tunnel, when I noticed—or got the feeling—something was beside me. Thinking it was one of the dogs, I said in a not-too-pleasant voice, "What are you doing here?" I don't let the dogs in the field with me when I'm using poison or traps, but sometimes they crawl under the fence. Anyway, I looked up, and there was a little person standing there with kind of a shocked look. I just got out the word "Oops," and I was going to add, *I didn't mean you*, when there was a blur, and the person was gone. I said, "I'm sorry," a little under my breath.

A couple of minutes later at another mole tunnel, I looked up, and the same little person was watching me. I smiled and said that I didn't mean to be rude, that I thought one of the dogs had got into the field. The little person said, "I heard the 'sorry.' That's why I came back." The little person added, "My mother told me that you could be a little unpleasant at times." I immediately stopped what I was doing and looked more intently.

I thought the little person had looked familiar. The resemblance to Sara was uncanny, but I thought that Davey was the only boy in the family, and I thought this little person was a boy because of the clothes and the bow. I asked, "Is Sara your mother?" and the little person said yes. I said, "I thought Davey was the only boy in the family." And at that, the little person got an angry look, kinda red, and then just stood there and kind of shook real fast and at the same time made a buzzing sound. It dawned on me that the person was talking so fast, I couldn't understand what was said.

Then the little person reached up and removed the hat, and all this hair fell out and around her shoulders, and I realized that this was no little boy but a beautiful, fully mature young woman. Feeling like a fool, I immediately said that I was sorry again and that it must be my day for using that word. I added that I remembered then that Davey had said he had two sisters, but I didn't know one was older than him. She quit shaking and buzzing and just stood there, still with the angry look on her face. Now, if it's one thing I know, good-looking, young, and probably spoiled teenage girls do not take kindly to being called boys. In fact, I could guarantee that this one didn't, and if looks could kill, I would have been in a lot of trouble. As it was, I figured that if she took that bow off of her shoulder, I was going to run for the house—as if that would do any good.

I asked her what her name was, and she said it was Darcy. She immediately added that she didn't know why she told me because she didn't like me very much. I almost said *Neither does your mother*, but I thought I had better keep my mouth shut on that. I said, "You must be older than Davey," and she just gave me a dumb look for a second and I thought I'd done it again.

Then she answered, "Well, I guess. I'm seventeen years old."

I said that my name was Wayne, and she made the comment, "That's a no-brainer. Everybody around here knows that." I thought, *Boy, do I have trouble talking to little people females. Either they take everything I say wrong, or they all have some serious attitude problems.* Personally, I thought it was the latter. I also wondered where she had picked up that slang phrase, "no-brainer." That's something that I have heard used on TV, but it wasn't common. I thought, *I suppose now that one of the little people is going to tell me that they have television.* I was definitely not going to believe that.

Darcy asked me what I was doing, and I told her that I was trying to poison moles. She couldn't understand why I was trying to kill the moles. I explained that I didn't like the molehills and that they killed some of the fruit trees in the orchard. I wasn't sure if they chewed the roots or just dug the dirt away from them, but they had dried out, causing the tree to die. Darcy told me that her people did not like poison very much. I could understand that, since I thought the little people more or less lived off the land. I said that if her people grew gardens, they wouldn't like moles any better than I did. She replied that they didn't have gardens; they acquired the fruit and vegetables that they needed from my garden and other fields that farmers grew. She was grinning when she said that. I looked up at her and said, "That is stealing, you know."

And she answered, "Not really. We do things for you, you just don't know about it." Then she added, "By the way, we will take care of your mole problem. Just don't use any more poison, OK?" I thought for a moment and then agreed. I didn't like bending down and digging out tunnels anyway; it killed my back.

I asked her how they were going to get rid of the moles. She said, "Just wait, and come out to the field when it's almost dark." I could watch and understand then. I was extremely curious but thought that I had better not push it. I would probably find out that evening.

It was around five thirty in the evening; I was cooking supper. I always ate a little early because Linda didn't get home from work until about seven or seven thirty. Anyway, I remembered what Darcy had said and realized that it was going to be dark in an hour or so. I turned the stove off and walked out to the field. The dogs went with me, and the cat followed along too. I got to the main fence and stood around, but I couldn't see anything happening anywhere. I had been there for around five minutes and was just getting ready to go back and finish cooking, when I turned and all of a sudden, the field was full of little people. Now, I mean *full* of little people. I didn't count, but there must have been thirty or more. I just stood there with my mouth hanging open. They were all standing absolutely still with either a bow drawn or what they call a "blowtube" held up to the mouth. I thought most of the women had blowtubes, but it was hard to tell because they dressed so similar.

At first, I couldn't tell what they were doing; they were all aiming their weapons down at the ground. Then I saw one of them shoot a bow. I looked closer at one that was standing near me, and then I understood. They had dug a small hole in the ground, apparently in a mole tunnel, waiting for a mole to appear. And when it did, they shot it. I could hear a slight noise like they were all whistling; it appeared as if they were calling the moles.

One of the little people looked over at me and waved, and I waved back. He walked over to me. It was Jamie. He said, "Hi, Wayne, Understand you don't like the moles much." I told him not really, and I appreciated the help. He explained that they didn't have to kill many. That they would leave the dead ones in the tunnels, and it would keep most of the others away for a while. He said that after all, they felt a little obligated to help out, since they had taken some things out of my orchard and garden the last few years, and he sure didn't want me to think they were thieves. At that, he just stood there and grinned. I grinned back and turned a little red. I told him that I shouldn't have mentioned anything to his daughter about it. He just laughed, saying, "And females can be a little funny about some things," and winked.

I said, "That's for sure," and then wondered what Darcy had told him I said.

About that time, I heard a car coming down the road; Jamie heard it too and said, "We will be back in a minute." He added, "Make that darn cat go home, or some of the women and children probably won't come back." Then they all just disappeared. I was getting used to this disappearing thing, but I still couldn't understand how any animal or person could move so fast.

I thought of what Jamie said and looked at Noodles, our cat, who was sitting next to me, looking out into the field. His tail was swinging back and forth, and he had that funny look in his eyes. Neither was a good sign; it usually indicated he was up to something. I clapped my hands and chased him back to the house; Mercy went after him, figuring it was a game.

I had just got back to the fence when all the little people appeared again. I hadn't noticed, but apparently the car was out of sight. I asked Jamie where they all went, and he said, "Oh, just over behind those trees," and pointed to the trees behind the barn.

I asked him how late they were going stay out in the field, and he said not much longer, just till dark, and that it should be long enough anyway. I said that I could understand the bow killing a mole, but I told him that the little blowgun darts didn't seem like they were big enough. Jamie looked at me and laughed. He said the women usually use the mouth tubes, that they put different types of toxic potions on the darts, depending on what they are using them for. He said the men sometimes use the potions on their arrows, but they have to get them from the women. I said that it looked to me like the females in his society had a lot of power. He looked around real quick to see if anybody was listening and then said quietly, "Too damned much." I thought, *Uh oh, I hit on a sore spot*. He added that it had always been that way, that the women were in the leadership positions and guarded most all of the clan secrets, like potions and medicines. He said about all the men did was the hard work—hunting, fishing, and making babies. At the last part of that comment, he started to laugh and then looked around again to see if anyone was listening.

I had a feeling that Jamie and his wife had been in an argument or disagreement previously. He seemed to have his nose out of joint over something. They had probably been arguing about me. Darcy had probably gone home and told her mother how much of an ass I was. I doubt very much that Sara disagreed with her.

I had noticed at least one thing for sure about the little people. Not only were they quick moving and talking when they wanted to be; they were also quick to get mad, and the opposite—quick to laugh. Also, I noticed that nothing really frightened them much but big birds, and they were extremely scared of them. If a little person was out in the open, he or she was always looking up and was usually armed with a bow or blowgun.

What made me think of this was while Jamie was standing there talking to me, not only was he looking all around, he was looking up, appearing a little fearful. I asked him about it. He said the only real things that they were scared of were big birds and cats, and both of them could sneak up on them before they were aware of it. He added, "And, of course, our wives," looking over at me and laughing. He said, "No, really," becoming serious, "big birds and cats can actually catch us and sometimes kill us."

CHAPTER 9

I never could really understand how the little people could exist without being seen and everybody knowing about them. I remember hearing stories about little people in Ireland and other places, but I thought they were fairy tales or made-up stories for children. Maybe that is how they have kept secret for so long.

My point is, if everyone is brought up believing a certain way—like, there is no such thing as Superman, Spiderman, fairies, or little people, that these are all just cartoon or storybook characters, then when an encounter does happen, well, we don't believe our eyes. In other words, we think it's a figment of our imagination. Instead of really seeing a little person, we rationalize and assume that we saw a raccoon, a squirrel, a cat, or some other little critter. I know that happened to me at first. The little people move so fast that unless they want you to really see them, you are not going to.

To prove a point, one day I was standing in the field behind the house, by an area that was covered with water. It had been raining hard for a couple days, and there were two or three inches of water standing over approximately an acre. There was no wind, but all of a sudden, a little whirlwind appeared on the water's surface, directly across from me. It came right at me. It was no big thing; I've seen air currents on water all my life—most people have—so I never thought anything of it until it got to me. And all of a sudden, Davey was standing right there. He startled me, and I sat right down in the mud. It was a good thing I had my rain pants on. Anyway, he said, "Hi, Wayne, what's up?" and started laughing. I didn't think it was funny, and I told him so. Before I could get up, another little whirlwind came across the water, and all of a sudden there was Darcy, standing there laughing. That was enough. Up and out of there I went. I could still hear them laughing when I got to the faucet to hose off. They sounded like two little chipmunks.

After a couple of minutes, they were standing right beside me. Davey said, "I'm sorry, Wayne, I didn't mean to scare you." I immediately informed him that I might have been surprised a little, but I wasn't scared. Darcy was looking at me, biting her cheeks and trying not to laugh again, while I attempted to get all the mud off.

I told them, "You know, I have seen you and your parents do a lot of different things, but I had no idea that you could walk on water."

Both started laughing, and Darcy said, "We can't. You should know better than that. Nobody can walk on water, and they would sink." I thought, *I know of one person that could*, but I didn't say anything.

Anyway, Davey said, "Wayne, we run real fast to stay on the surface. We don't weigh much, and as long as we keep moving fast, we are OK." After I thought about it for a minute, it did seem logical. They didn't weigh much, in fact, and I remember that while I was sitting in the mud, they didn't seem to be muddy at all.

I said, "I know you can run real fast. In fact, I don't see how a big bird can catch you." Both the kids turned a little pale and looked up into the sky. Darcy gave me a funny look and disappeared.

Davey said, "We can't hear them coming. They catch us when we're standing still." He said, "That's how I lost one of my little sisters last year." I felt like a fool for bringing it up. That must have been the reason that Darcy left so suddenly. I turned to Davey and told him that I was sorry; I didn't know. He answered that it was all right. "Like Mother always tells us, death is part of life, but I sure hate those darn birds." He then added that he had better get home and said good-bye. I said good-bye and to say hello to his parents as he disappeared.

I could just about kick myself. It seemed like I was always saying or asking the wrong thing. If I was learning one thing, it was that it was easy for little people to laugh, but it was easy to hurt their feelings too. They seemed to be very sensitive.

I was becoming very protective of my new friends. Not only was I trying to keep their existence a total secret, but I was developing a real hate for eagles—what they call "big birds." Don't get me wrong; I wasn't to the point of going out and shooting eagles. I would probably end up in jail, and that wouldn't help matters at all. There just had to be some way to deter the birds without killing them. I'm sure if it was known that eagles preyed on little people, there wouldn't be an eagle left. Most people would become very protective, just like I did. Now, I have seen eagles catch ducks, rabbits, and other small animals. I even saw pictures of an eagle flying off with a small dog, one time. It's not uncommon to see an eagle flying in Alaska with a ten- or fifteen-pound salmon in its talons, so there is no doubt in my mind that one could pick up a five- or ten-pound little person and fly off. I'm not even going to describe how they killed those animals and birds when they got to a tree. I saw the whole thing, and I don't really want to think about it. I will say that I have always thought that an eagle is one of the most brutal creatures in the wildlife kingdom, but that's just my opinion.

CHAPTER 10

Up to this time, I still don't really know that much about the little people, as I call them. It seems that every time I start asking questions, I either kind of insult them or hurt their feelings. And in Sara's case, she usually gets mad at me.

They really don't seem that much different from us, except they are smaller. Their voices are higher pitched, but that's probably because of their size. (Actually, I've heard people our size with voices almost as high as theirs.) I have touched them, and their skin felt like ours. I did notice their skin felt a little hot, but not that much different.

They all have brown eyes; at least the ones that I've noticed. But remember, I've only seen maybe five or six up close. I did notice different shades of brown though.

I didn't notice any of them with light hair—I mean, with blond or red hair. I have seen some with gray or white hair. In fact, Jamie has white hair and a white beard, but he doesn't seem that old.

I'm very curious how they can travel so fast. I know they don't weigh very much, and I have no idea of the reason for that. But for sure, they don't need cars to get anywhere in a hurry. And another thing: I have never seen any of them breathing hard from running.

I think they trust me, up to a point. They seem to be testing me with just a little bit of information about themselves every once in a while. They're probably watching me to see if I can keep their secret. I don't see them that often either, maybe once every two weeks or so. I get a feeling they are around me a lot more than that, but they try not to let me know. When they do let me see them, it usually startles me. I mean, like, I'll be working on something like the tractor, and I'll turn around to get a tool, and one of them will be standing there watching me. Wow, talk about startled. Sometimes I don't take it too well.

I know there is no reason to be scared of them. I am almost positive they wouldn't hurt me, although there is no doubt in my mind that if they wanted to, I would be in a pile of hurt.

As I stated before, they seem to be a little back-woodsy, but you wouldn't know it by talking to them. They seem to have a high degree of intelligence and gifts that are even beyond ours. I mean, just think about it for a minute. Here is a race of people that subsist on hunting and gathering and make their own clothes by hand, yet they have the knowledge to heal almost instantly. Also, I don't believe they have any enemies, with the exception of the eagles. It really doesn't sound like a bad life to me, but then, like I said before, I don't really know that much about them yet.

It had been about a month since I had seen any of them, when one morning my wife and I were driving to town and noticed property-for-sale signs in the field just down the road from our house. I was rather surprised. The sign said 250 Acres and gave the real estate agent's name and phone number. I wrote it down, and when we got back home, I called him. I found out that the sale included the field and woods behind my property, where the little people were supposed to live. I was a little worried, but I didn't mention anything to Linda. I didn't want her jumping all over me or teasing me about the little people again.

It couldn't have been two days later that I heard some small voices behind the barn, and when I got there, I found Jamie and Sara. Jamie said, "We've been waiting for you. We knew you were in the barn and figured that you would hear our voices." I asked them why they didn't come to the house and knock on the door when they wanted to talk to me.

They both just stared at me for a second, and then Sara said, "Oh, sure, and then we would have to take care of your wife when she passes out on the floor." I laughed about that and told her she was probably right.

I added, "You know, it really wouldn't hurt for me to introduce you to her, one of these days. I'm sure everything would turn out OK if she was expecting it."

Sara said, "Well, maybe sometime. But not now. The real reason that we wanted to talk to you was to find out why you want to sell your property."

I answered that it wasn't my property, and I was just as surprised as they were that it was for sale. I told them that I had talked to the real estate agent and what I had found out about the price and property lines and such. Then I asked what they and their little group would do if the property was sold. Jamie answered, "If you mean my family, we wouldn't do anything." He looked at me a little funny and said, "I don't know if I told you, but all of us that live over in those woods"—and he pointed to the trees across the field—"are related. They are my father, mother, brothers, and their families."

He pointed out that his earlier ancestors had moved into those woods a hundred or so years ago and that they had never had any problems. He then added, "Besides, my people have lived around here for thousands of years, long before you bigger people ever came around." I thought, *Good grief, I know where this is heading.* He said, "But you know, Wayne, we will move to a different location before we will let anyone know of our existence." I didn't really know what to tell them, so I offered that another farmer would probably buy the land and everything would probably stay the same. Although in my mind, I had a suspicion somebody might buy the property just to build a house in the treed area where the little people lived. I told them that I would keep in contact with the agent and let them know anything that I found out.

After they said good-bye and left, I sat down on the old stump and thought about the situation. I made up my mind what to do, but I had to talk to Linda first. Before I got up and left, Jamie came back. He said that he thought he should tell me something. He went on to explain why Sara was reluctant to meet Linda. He said that every time in the past when females of his people came in contact with females of my people, things just didn't work out very well. It seemed, he thought, that the size difference caused all the problems. The bigger females had a tendency to "mother" females of his size. In other words, they treated them like children, and of course, his people didn't like it. He said, "Contact with one of your females hasn't taken place for a long time." Not in his lifetime, anyway.

I asked, "By the way, Jamie, how old are you?" and he told me forty-five.

He grinned and said, "Bet you thought I was a lot older because of my white hair, huh?" He said that he had always had white hair, from birth. He added, "Wayne, my people live a lot longer than your people, unless we get killed or die from some weird disease that our women can't heal. It is not uncommon for us to live well over two hundred years, and in fact, my great-grandfather is still alive and well. He remembers when your people came to this country. He is always telling us stories about the Indians that lived here before." My God, I was flabbergasted. I asked if maybe someday I could talk to him. He said, "Sure, he would probably really like that; he doesn't do much of anything anymore but talk anyway," and started laughing. Now, I'm kind of a history buff, and I think that would be really cool. Just think, talking and hearing about things that happened over two hundred years ago with somebody who was actually there. Anyway, Jamie said he had to go and left.

I went back to the house and decided to talk to Linda about my idea. She was home, not at work. First let me explain something. We are not rich people, but we do own some property on the Oregon coast that we were thinking about selling. We had not decided what to do with the money once we did. We had talked about moving back to the coast or buying a rental house and other options, but we hadn't made up our minds.

Now, my wife is not very amenable to change or new ideas, so when I first brought up the notion of buying some of the property behind the house, she of course said no. I explained to her that if we could obtain around sixty additional acres, our property would be worth a lot more when we did sell our house, and it would give us more to retire on. I did not tell her about the other reason: Jamie and his family. Anyway, she finally said she would think about it when the time came.

Meanwhile, we went to the county planning office and got the OK to split off sixty acres of the seller's land if the owner agreed to it. I contacted the real estate agent and asked him if the owner would consider selling off a piece of the property. He stated he would contact the owner and call me later, which he did two weeks later. The answer was no. My wife, always the optimist, said,

"Wait until we have the money in hand, and then let's see if he turns it down."

I decided to wait for a while before I told Jamie what we were trying to do. I didn't see any reason to get him and his family's hopes up in case things didn't work out.

CHAPTER II

It was one of those beautiful days in June, the kind of day when a person can see forever. Linda had already left for work, and I was working in the garden. I was really pleased with my garden this year. All the plants were above ground and doing well. I planted a little more this year, knowing now that I was feeding a few more mouths than Linda's and mine. I wasn't upset about it; in fact, I was rather pleased. Actually, I would have never known that the little people had taken some vegetables out of the garden if they hadn't told me. For some reason, they don't leave tracks in the dirt, probably because they don't weigh much and due to the soft moccasin type of shoes they wear. I don't think they took much anyway.

Now, the orchard was a different thing. I did notice some fruit missing last year, but I just figured that the birds got them. There was one tree in particular that I recall. It had real small apples that when ripe and stored in the refrigerator lasted three or four months. It was no big deal, but I thought that someday I would ask Jamie about it, just out of curiosity.

About midmorning, while I was hoeing around the corn plants, I heard the most ungodly noises coming from behind the barn. Actually, the commotion seemed quite some distance away, not close. I couldn't see out into the field, of course because the barn was in the way. It seemed to be whistles and screeches, high pitched and loud.

I dropped the hoe and started to run around the barn so I could see. Bruno and Mercy were going crazy, and I mean crazy. Mercy was barking and running around in a circle. Bruno was roaring, and just as I got to the gate at the side of the barn, he ran right around me, almost knocking me down, and then jumped that five-foot gate. My God, I couldn't figure out what was going on.

I got around the barn and through the brush so I could see. Bruno was already halfway across the field; Mercy had just gone past me into it. Both dogs were still barking. I could see two big birds, undoubtedly eagles, circling just above treetop level across the field. They were trying to gain altitude, but one of them had a hold of something pretty good sized and was having trouble flying. I started running across the field, screaming and waving my arms. I knew what I was looking at. That damned bird had grabbed a little person.

The eagle was full-grown and mature with a white head, and it was huge. He had the little person by the back—the upper back, just below the shoulders. The little person was thrashing around with his arms and legs, apparently trying to get loose or hit the eagle.

I had just got to the other side of the field, out of breath. There were little people everywhere. Some were yelling, and others were blowing some kind of a whistle that made a very high, loud, penetrating noise. I got an instant headache; it must have been from the whistle. The dogs were barking and jumping in the air.

Jamie all of a sudden was right beside me. He had his bow in his hand, as did some of the others. "We can't shoot, it's too far, and we would probably hit Darcy," he said.

I yelled, "Darcy! Is that Darcy?" He answered yes. He had tears running down his cheeks. I yelled "Shit!" or some other cuss word, I don't remember. Anyway, the two birds started angling across the field the way I had come.

I started running back as fast as I could. When I got to the gate by the barn, I lost sight of the birds. I ran for the house to get my .22 rifle. Meanwhile, Bruno went flying by me, heading across the highway and into the trees, the direction the birds had flown. I got my rifle and went right after him as fast as I could go. I couldn't hear any more noise except Bruno barking and me crashing through the brush. I was throwing all caution to the wind and getting pretty scratched and cut up doing it.

I stopped to catch my breath, and it seemed that Bruno's barking was getting farther away toward the river. I thought, *That bird is trying to get to its nest.* Most of the eagles in our area have nests near the river. Then it dawned on me what that bird was planning to do. It must have little ones in that nest. Lord, I got half sick at my stomach and took off running again as fast as I could. I think I had tears in my eyes. Anyway, I didn't see the old wire fence that was about knee-high. I went down hard, rolled over, and thought, *I'm not going to help anyone if I end up breaking a leg or something.* I got up, made myself calm down and took off again, using a little more caution.

All of a sudden, it seemed like Bruno was barking just ahead of me. We weren't near the river yet, and I didn't think there were any eagle nests this close to my house. I slowed down and looked up into the trees, but I couldn't see anything. I wondered where all the little people were at. As fast as they could run, I figured they would all have been in front of me with Bruno.

I came around a bunch of brush, and there was Bruno, barking and jumping up at the base of a big fir tree. He was in a frenzy; he was even biting at the bark on the tree. I had never seen that dog like that ever. I didn't really want to get near him. I couldn't see up to the top of the tree anyway, so I started backing up to get a better view from a different angle.

There was a small clearing about twenty feet away, so I ran over to it and got myself into a position to see most of the top portion of the tree—which was a long way up there, I might add. I saw movement and threw my rifle up. My God, my hair was up on the back of my neck. That damned eagle was on a limb at the top of the tree. It was jerking its head back and forth and up and down, I couldn't see Darcy, and I was afraid I was too late. I know from prior experience: that is how eagles kill their prey.

I backed up to a tree, put my scope on nine power, the highest magnification, and took a rest on a big limb that was sticking out.

I could see the eagle clearly now. He had Darcy pinned down with one foot and was holding onto the limb with the other. She was still alive and fighting the eagle off with a stick or knife or something. My God, was she fighting. There was blood all over her and the eagle. The only chance she had is if I could hit that eagle. Good grief, they were moving all over, the limb was bouncing up and down, and the limb that I had the rifle resting on was moving all over—and I was supposed to hit that bird without hitting Darcy.

It was a long shot to the top of that tree with a .22 rifle. Of course, the bird wouldn't hold still. I put the cross hairs on the bird's chest and waited for a couple of seconds, hoping the bird would stop. It did, holding its head up, looking all around like it sensed something, and I pulled the trigger.

Boy, all hell busted loose when I did that. The eagle had its wings spread out while trying to kill Darcy, so when I hit it, it flapped its wings, fast. Both it and Darcy fell, and it looked like the whole top of the tree was coming down. I figured Darcy must be unconscious because she was falling like a wet rag from one limb to another. The eagle, on the other hand, was not dead. It looked like it was trying to catch up to the little girl.

They had fallen about halfway down the tree when I dropped the rifle and ran over. I had just got there when

I saw Darcy falling from the last limb, with the eagle right behind her. I dove to catch her before she hit the ground, and just as I got hold of her, something hit me on the back of my head.

The next thing that I remember was hearing little voices from a long way off. One was saying, "Roll him over so I can see the cuts on the back of his head."

Then another said, "He's waking up, he's starting to move."

I opened my eyes and saw Sara kneeling down beside me, looking right into my face. She asked, "How do you feel?"

I said, "Well, I've felt better, but I'm all right I guess." She had tears in her eyes and bent over and hugged my head and kissed me on the cheek.

She said, "Thank you, Wayne." I looked up and noticed that I was surrounded by little people, and they were all smiling.

My memory was coming back. I said, "Darcy..." and started to get up.

Sara pushed me back down. "Darcy is just fine. She had a terrible time. She was close to death when I got here, in fact, and you were in pretty poor shape too." I told her that I couldn't remember what happened after I caught Darcy, before she hit the ground.

Jamie was one of the little people standing beside me. He said, "I think you missed out on a real mess. We missed it too, and we never got here in time." I started to ask why when he said, "You know, we can't run fast in the trees and brush. That's why you got here long before we did." Well, that answered that question. He added,

"Boy, you sure plowed the brush down. It has taken Sara a long time just healing all the scratches and cuts on your body, let alone the bad cut and damage to your head the eagle caused."

I looked over at him and said, "What?"

He said, "Oh, you don't know about all that, do you?"

Jamie said that one of his people got there just as I caught Darcy, and the eagle hit me. He witnessed the whole thing. He said that when I caught her and tried to shield her, the eagle tried to kill me by biting the back of my neck and beating me with its wings. He said that Bruno saved my life by grabbing the eagle around the neck with his jaws. Apparently, there was a terrible fight. Both the eagle and Bruno were covered in blood when Mercy arrived and attacked the bird from behind. The bird turned toward Mercy and Bruno struck, taking the eagle's head clear off. Then, Jamie said, the dogs literally tore the bird apart. "There are feathers and pieces of it everywhere."

Sara said that neither Darcy nor I would have lasted long if she hadn't gotten here when she did, and that we both were in bad shape. Darcy had put up a valiant fight, but the bird would have eventually won. The bird had opened her stomach, and her arms were gashed very badly from fending the bird off. She had lost a lot of blood. I started to get up, but she told me to lie still and that I could see Darcy pretty soon. She sounded like she meant business, but in a nice sort of way, so I lay back down.

Sara said that it takes a while for the healing agent to work and that I had to lie still until it was finished.

She continued saying that I had not been much better off than Darcy. That the cuts and bruises on my body were nothing compared to what the bird did to the back of my neck. She said, "I'm not going to describe it to you. I'll just say you wouldn't have made it much longer."

About that time, I felt a pressure on my right leg. I looked down, and there was Bruno, laying his head on my leg. Gosh, he was still covered with blood, but I couldn't see any bad injuries. He did have a lot of that yellow or gold stuff on him that I had seen Sara use before. I thought, *That stuff must work on dogs, and everything*; I even noticed it on my hands. I imagined that it was all over my face and the back of my head and neck too. It seemed that everything felt warm and tingly. In fact, I was getting to feel pretty good.

I reached down to put my hand on Bruno's head, but he was gone. I looked over at Jamie, and he said, "Oh, he goes back and forth between you and Darcy to make sure you two are OK." I grinned and asked if he had been hurt bad. He said yes, "But not life threatening like you and Darcy." He went on to say that the reason the eagle attacked me was that he thought I was taking his prey away. He said they get very possessive with their food this time of year because they are nesting. I said my God, I believe that.

Sara said, "You can sit up now, Wayne. You might feel a little dizzy. Does the back of your head and neck feel tight?" I said yes, and a little hot and tingly too. She answered that it was skin and tissue knitting back together. She added, "I wasn't sure the healing agent would work very well on you, you had such extreme damage, and you are a big person. But it looks good to me. Here, take this and chew it," and she handed me a piece of something out of a little bag. It looked like a piece of tree bark and tasted bitter. I made a face, and she grinned. She said, "I know it doesn't taste very good, but you need it. It will heal the inside of you; I think your people call it shock." I knew what she meant. I was shaking like a leaf, but it quit in about five minutes or less.

I was still sitting down, facing Jamie, and we were talking when Jamie looked over my shoulder and said, "Somebody wants to talk to you." I started to turn around very slowly; I was scared to move very fast. And there was Darcy, standing there without a stitch of clothes on. She was almost totally covered with the gold powder, and she was glowing. Her hair was hanging down, and she looked like a beautiful little doll, literally—just like a porcelain doll that one of my daughters had when they were young. Although, I might add, this little doll had breasts and other things that porcelain dolls don't have. I know that my face had probably turned red, but nobody could tell because I had that stuff on my face too. All the little people were still standing around us, and none of them seemed one bit concerned that she was totally naked, so I presumed it was a common thing in their society.

She looked at her mom, who said, "It's OK now," and with that, Darcy threw her arms around my neck and gave me a big hug.

Backing up again with tears running down her face, she said, "Oh, thank you, Wayne," and hugged me again.

This time she just hung on and cried. I found myself crying too.

About that time, Bruno walked through the little people and licked my face. I looked over, and all the little people were crying or laughing, and some doing both at the same time. I started laughing a little, and Darcy backed up with grin on her face. She said, "You didn't have to do that. You almost died. But I'm sure glad you came after me. I will always be indebted to you, I owe you my life."

I heard her father behind me say, "We all owe you, Wayne."

I looked at Darcy and said, "I appreciate it, but I don't think anyone owes me anything. There is no doubt in my mind that I wouldn't be here alive right now, if it wasn't for your mother." I looked over at Sara, who was grinning, tears running down her cheeks. At that, all the little people grouped around me and hugged me and Darcy and each other and laughed, and everybody had tears running down their faces.

All of a sudden, Davey appeared with some extra clothes for Darcy. He ran right to his sister, dropped the clothes, and gave her a big hug. He looked at me and grinned. I found out later that he had been one of the first to arrive on the scene. He had been so worried about his sister that Sara had made him go back home and get Darcy the clothes. Apparently, the eagle had ripped the ones she was wearing to shreds.

I stood up and about fell over. I felt pretty dizzy, but it gradually went away. Looking around, I could see what Jamie was talking about. What a mess. Blood, feathers, and dog hair all over the place. I saw the eagle's body and went over to see if I had actually hit it, but there was no way to tell. There wasn't much left of it.

Everybody started back home, and the dogs and I followed along. They were going slow, which was just fine with me; I still didn't feel up to par yet. I had never seen them walk slowly before. It looked like a whole bunch of little kids walking along, dodging limbs and trees and jabbering. It looked kind of cute, for lack of a better word, and I just stumbled along and chuckled.

When we got to the road and out into the open, the little people started to disappear. Jamie was the last to leave. He told me good-bye and said we would be talking soon.

I walked the dogs across the road and over to our place. We went right to the garden hose, and I'm glad it was warm because I washed both dogs and myself. Boy, what a mess we were, all covered with blood and the gold stuff that Sara put on us. Over by the back porch, I took all my clothes off and went in to take a shower. I noticed that all my underclothes were totally soaked with blood, presumably mine, and when I got under the shower, wow, the shower stall was full of blood. I checked my body all over in the shower, and when I dried off, but I could find no open wounds. I did notice red spots on me that still felt hot and tingly.

I dressed and went back outside to sack up all my bloody, ripped clothes in a garbage bag and deposited them in the garbage can. I noticed both dogs were lying down, asleep on the lawn already. I went over and checked Bruno out. There were no visible wounds, although I could see places where chunks of hair were missing. Mercy looked fine too, but I didn't see any hair missing on her.

I looked all around and couldn't see anything out of place, so I went back into the house, lay down on the lounge, and took a nap.

Linda came home around six o'clock and woke me up. She looked at me kinda funny because I never sleep that time of day. She said, "Hi honey, how was your day?"

I said, "Oh, just fine."

She said, "Your hair feels wet. Did you take a shower?"

"Oh, yes, I gave the dogs a bath and got myself all wet and stinky, so I took a shower and fell asleep on the lounge."

"Oh."

I got the subject changed to how her day had gone and kept the conversation off of me. I thought, *Boy, if she only knew*.

The next day after Linda went to work, I heard the dogs bark, so I went out the back door. Standing up against the house was my rifle. Good grief, I had forgotten all about my rifle. I had never picked it up when I left the woods the day before. One of the little people must have brought it back to me. I heard Bruno whine, and looking over at him, I noticed him looking toward the field. I tried to see what he was looking at when I noticed Davey step out from behind a bush and wave. Then he just disappeared.

CHAPTER 12

About two days after the eagle experience, Darcy suddenly appeared in front of me while I was working in the garden. She looked different. I couldn't put my finger on it. She looked cleaner, fresher, or something like that. Then it dawned on me. She looked happier. She was jumping around, laughing and grinning, which made me laugh too.

I asked, "What has got into you today? You can't seem to stand still."

She said, laughing, "I have a surprise for you. Some of my friends will be here soon, and we are all going for a walk." I looked at her, and she added, "Oh, of course, at your speed, not fast," and grinned great big.

I said, "You mean, you are taking me for a walk."

"Yup." And she laughed some more.

About that time, little people started popping up all around me. When Darcy showed up, I had been kneeling down in the dirt, pulling weeds, so I was at about their height. I found myself surrounded by five giggling little people. In fact, they all looked like young girls, like Darcy.

Now, this did not appear to be a good situation. I knew that the little people loved to play pranks on each other and on big people sometimes too, including me. All kinds of things were going through my mind, and I guess they could see the anxiety in my face because they really started laughing then. Darcy said, between fits of laughter, "Wayne, you look a little scared. Now how could my big hero be scared of six little girls like us?"

I had had about enough of this and was in the process of standing up and heading to the house when they all grabbed my arms and held me down, and then each one of them kissed me on the cheek. Darcy said, "I told my friends how soft you were, and since they had never touched a big person, they wanted to find out for themselves." She added, "You are considered a hero among my people, and you are just lucky that kissing your cheek is all these girls do to you." I know my expression changed, and I started to move. So she continued real fast, saying, "But I talked them out of it. You big people are such prudes." I thought, *Young people are the same everywhere.*

She said that her dad wanted her and the girls to bring me to their home. He had told her that it was time that I saw where they lived. She said that they were going to treat it like a holiday. I really didn't know what I was in for, but I decided to go along with it. What else could I do?

Darcy and another little girl took me by the hand, and with the other four leading, away we went. All the girls were talking and laughing, and the four in front kept zipping away and back again. We had gotten about halfway around the back field when it dawned on me that there were a lot more little people in the group than there were when we started out. In fact, I was surrounded by little people of all ages, some who looked really old, and everybody was laughing and trying to touch me. One thing that I had previously noticed was little people touching each other all the time. Now, it appeared that I was included too. It seemed that they were touching me anywhere they could reach. One time we stopped, and a couple of little people put their faces on the backs of my hands. By the looks in their faces, I got the feeling that they kind of adored me, or at least felt affection toward me. It gave me a weird feeling—but a good feeling, I might add.

We got to the back of the field, next to a bunch of fir trees, and stopped. All of a sudden, the thick brush just opened up. I had never seen anything quite like it. There were no ropes, gates, or anything. The brush just moved aside and revealed a path that I could see going back into the trees. I had to bend over to follow the little people, but not too much. We went about a hundred feet or so and walked around a slight bend when I saw their homes. My God, it was just cute, I don't know how else to describe it. It was just like out of a storybook. The homes were about six feet tall and had moss and straw roofs. They were about ten feet square, except one of them that was a lot bigger, probably twenty foot square.

There were little people everywhere, some walking, and some sitting on the ground and on stools. They all seemed to be laughing, or at least grinning, and most of them were watching me approach.

One of them was waving, and I recognized Jamie. He was standing by a small fire. There was something roasting over the fire; it looked like a large bird. I walked up to him and said, "Good Lord, Jamie, don't tell me that is an eagle."

You would have thought that I had told the biggest joke in the world. There were little people, including Jamie, falling down laughing all around me. When Jamie could finally talk, he stood up and said, "No, but don't think we haven't tried. They are just too darned tough," and that started everyone laughing again.

Sara came up to me, took my arm and hugged it to her cheek, and said, "Hi, Wayne, welcome to our homes." Now, that about floored me. Sara never seemed to like me much, but I could tell she really meant what she said. I thanked her and put my hand on her shoulder. She smiled up at me, great big, and touched my hand with hers. It gave me a warm feeling.

Now, I'm no fool. I knew they were taking a big chance by bringing me here to their homes. I thought, *There is no way that I would betray their trust.* I would protect them with my life, just like I would my own family.

I felt Sara squeezing my hand, and I looked back over at her. She was beaming all over and I thought, good grief, I suppose now they are going to tell me they can read my thoughts. Sara looked up at me with a twinkle in her eyes and said "No, not everyone can. But I can when I'm touching you." My God, I about fell over. I know I blushed because I remember thinking some thoughts I wouldn't want any of them to hear or know about. Sara just burst out laughing and then came up close to me and said, "Don't worry, Wayne, I can keep secrets too."

I heard a commotion behind me and turned around. There was Bruno, lying on the ground with some very small little people all over him. They were all squealing and hugging him. I had no doubt that he had been here before. I gave him a stern look because I knew he had jumped the gate, and he knows that is a no-no. He immediately looked away from me, but I noticed he didn't get up.

I turned back to Jamie, and he said, "No, Wayne, this isn't an eagle. It's one of your neighbor's turkeys." The whole place started laughing again. He then added, "No, not your neighbor across the street, a neighbor a long ways off. He won't miss it. He has a lot of them, and they are always getting away. About half of the ones that get away are caught and eaten by coyotes, the other half by us." Then Jamie said, "Come with me, and I will show you around our place." He said, "Our homes may look like they have been here a long time, but they haven't. In fact, we can move really quick and make new ones if we have to. Everything the home is made from is natural and from the surrounding area. The walls from mud and straw, and the roof from sticks, straw, and moss. A lot of the home is under the ground; there are tunnels that lead from one place to another." There were large chambers that were used to store different kinds of food because it is cool in them all year.

Jamie took me over to one of the small buildings and opened the door so I could see inside. I had to bend down and get on my knees. I could see surprisingly well. There was light coming from small windows that I hadn't noticed before. It looked really cozy and clean, not what I expected. I might add, there was a nice smell that I can't really describe.

Jamie was in front of me, pointing to some small rooms off to one side. "These are bedrooms of the kids." Then crossing over to the other side of the main room, he pointed out a larger room, saying that it was Sara's and his bedroom. The large room in the center of the building looked like a lounging area; there were chairs, pillows, two small tables, and a number of other things that you would see in any other home. I didn't see any stove or kitchen and asked Jamie about it. He stated that there was no need for them, that all the cooking was done outside in a community cooking area—where the turkey was being roasted. I asked about heat in the winter, and he went over to a metal lid that was lying flat on the floor. He lifted it, revealing a large pot or metal chamber that looked like it was full of rocks. He said that in the winter, they heat a certain kind of rock outside and then transfer it to the heating chamber in the house. He added that it keeps the home warm and snug, even in the most severe winters and cold weather. He showed me one of the stones; it looked round, like what we call a "thunder egg." There was a metal ring apparently screwed into it. I looked up at Jamie with a quizzical look, and he explained that the ring was how they carried the stone when it was hot. He said the stone was not from around our area. It came from a long way off and is able to retain heat like no other stone. It came from a certain volcano here in Oregon. He said that as far as he knew, it was the only kind of stone that was used for heating and had been for many, many generations. Also, only that kind of stone is used all over the world by his people, as far as he knew. Needless to say, I was extremely impressed.

Jamie showed me all around their little village and introduced me to everybody. I didn't remember too many of their names or a lot that was said that day because one of the little men had run over to give me a small wooden cup, saying that it was for me. It was full of some kind of a sweet-smelling liquid. Jamie said it was what the men drank on special occasions and just grinned at me. Good grief, the first drink that I had from the little cup about knocked me on my butt. It was probably the strongest alcoholic drink that I ever had; at least, I think it was alcohol. Anyway, after drinking that small cup, I was floating everywhere, giggling and acting like an idiot. All the little people were laughing and having a good time. I remember seeing some of the men worse off than me, a lot worse. I think I ate half of that turkey; that drink they gave me made me ravenous. I just know I made a pig of myself.

Boy, was there a lot of food. Those little people can really eat. I think it is because they have a high metabolism. I never tasted anything that I didn't like. It was all just delicious.

Sometime during the afternoon, the little guy who had brought me my first drink brought me my fourth, fifth, or something like that. Anyway, I was eating the most fantastic-tasting piece of pie when I drained that cup and apparently fell over with a grin on my face. Anyway, that's what I was told later. I guess I was the life of the party because about twenty little men got to carry me home. I understand it was quite a merry situation; they all kept falling down giggling. They had brought a small jug of that drink with them, so when they did fall down, they would all sit around me and have another drink.

I woke up in the barn sometime later. There were little men lying on and around me everywhere. My God, can little people snore. I only know one person that can snore like that, a good friend of mine who lives on the Oregon coast.

Bruno was lying in the middle. I could have sworn he was grinning. I said something like, "Knock it off!" and got up. Lord, I had to get out of there, my head was killing me, and all that snoring was not helping. I headed to the house and lay back down on the lounge where it was quiet.

Linda got home a couple of hours later from work. She woke me up when she drove into the driveway. I jumped up, washed my mouth out, and straightened my clothes; I was covered with leaves and sawdust from the barn. I met her at the door. She looked at me and asked, "Do you feel all right? You don't look too good." I answered that I thought I might have a touch of the flu or something, that I had been lying on the lounge. She looked at me for a couple seconds more but didn't say anything else.

CHAPTER 13

About three weeks after my visit with Jamie and his family, I had a chance to meet his great-grandfather. I had walked out the back door of our house when I heard a little voice saying my name. At first I thought it was a bird chirping, but then I recognized my name, "Wayne," being said over and over again. I walked in the direction the voice was coming from and found a little person sitting on a limb in a tree in the backyard.

I stood under him, looking up for a second or two, then asked, "What are you doing up there?" He answered that he had been waiting for me and he didn't trust dogs too much, no matter what all his family said. I said, "Well, come on down, the dogs won't bother you." Which he did, dropping right in front of me, at my feet. I said, "Wow, you are pretty agile for a person your age." He looked up at me with a disgusted look and asked. What does age have to do with anything?"

"Well, I couldn't jump out of that tree like that. I would probably fall right on my face, and I think I'm a little younger than you."

He looked at me for a minute, and then he laughed and said, "A damned-sight lot younger, I'd bet."

About that time, Bruno came up behind him and licked him on the ear. He jumped toward me and turned, wiping his ear with his coat sleeve. "Ugh, damn, I hate that! See why I don't trust dogs? They are always sneaking around, trying to lick me." He was jumping around, shaking and rubbing his head and muttering, "Yuck!" and "Icky!" and some other words that I couldn't understand. Meanwhile, I about fell on the ground, I was laughing so hard. Bruno was just standing there grinning, like he had done that before and wasn't upset at all.

The little old man asked if I remembered him from the party at their homes. I told him that he looked familiar, but I couldn't remember his name. He said he was John and that he was the one giving me the stuff to drink that made me feel so good. I laughed and said, "Oh, yes, you are Jamie's great-grandfather." He said that was right, except he was Jamie's great-great-grandfather. I said, "Good grief, how old are you?"

"You're probably not going to believe me, but— around two hundred and forty, give or take a few years." He added that when you get that old, years kinda run together.

Linda had already gone to work, so I asked John to come into the house. He had seen Linda leave, so he agreed, although he was very hesitant. I don't think he had ever been in a big person's house before in all those years. He walked very cautious and soft, like he was sneaking. He looked all over with great big eyes, and as if he would disappear any moment—except I had closed the door behind us, and he couldn't. I chuckled to myself. He was trapped, and he knew it. I told him to sit in one of the big, soft chairs in the living room, but he kept walking around, looking at all the pictures, and muttering to himself. He was fascinated with the television. I think he thought it was a window because it appeared as if he was trying to see through it. Anyway, I picked up the remote and turned it on. And that was definitely not the thing to do.

My gosh, it felt like a bomb went off in the living room. Pictures were flying off the wall, lamps overturned, papers flying around in the air, and all the time a loud buzzing could be heard. I quickly turned the television off, and then all of a sudden, it just stopped.

Everything was settling down, and as I looked around, I saw a little face and two big eyes looking all over from underneath the coffee table. I didn't know whether to laugh or get angry, and then I decided not to do either one. Heaven knows what would have happened if I had.

He crawled out and stood up, brushing himself off. I asked, "Are you all right?"

He turned to me, his face all red, and said, "Of course. I just got a little startled there for a minute, and I can't get out. The doors are all closed."

"Why would you want to leave? You just got here, and I thought you wanted to talk to me."

"I don't think I want to talk to you now."

"Why not?"

He was looking at the television again and answered very hesitantly, "Because I don't want to end up in that box with those other people. Who are they, anyway? They are smaller than I am."

My God, I just about fell over. I asked John, "Haven't you ever seen a television before?"

"Well, yes, but I don't really know what they are used for, and now I don't think I want to know, either. I could see the one person screaming in pain in front of all those other people."

I immediately said, "No, the person was singing in front of an audience." And then I explained what a television really was. John seemed to be quite impressed and started to calm down.

I asked him what he came to see me about, and he told me that Jamie wanted him to come over, saying that I had some questions about the old days. I had totally forgotten that I had mentioned that to Jamie. Anyway, I said, "Oh, yes, I have gobs of questions, John. I mean, I would just love to know what this country was like a couple of hundred years ago."

"Well, that will probably take quite some time, and I've got a pretty busy schedule, you know." Then his eyes twinkled, and he chuckled. He added, "Not really. I don't think that I have ever had a busy schedule." I thought, *That's probably why he has lived so long.*

"John, just start telling me about things you can remember way back when you were young...let's see, about the turn of the nineteenth century...I guess you would have been around twenty or thirty years old then, right?"

John looked at me and said, "Wow, this might take some doing. I sure wish I had a bottle of that stuff we had at the party the other day. It kind of helps me remember things." Then he was quiet and just grinned at me. I caught the hint and got up, heading to the kitchen and saying I might have something just as good. Out of the cupboard, I got a bottle of scotch that I had had around for years and put a small amount in a glass. I didn't think John could drink too much because of his size and all. Boy, was I mistaken.

I handed John the glass; he smelled the contents, rolled his eyes, and drank it in one gulp. He belched, handed the glass back to me, and then grinned again. I just sat there staring at him, and then I asked, "Well, did that help your memory?"

"Some. At least enough to get me going." And he grinned some more. While I got up to refill his glass, John started talking. "Wayne," he said, "You wouldn't believe what it was like back then. It was real quiet and peaceful. All you big people were not around then. Oh, there were a few, you know, the dark-skinned, I think you call them Indians, right?" I told him that was correct. He went on, saying that his kind almost had the country to themselves. He said that there were no cars or paved roads. The only houses were those made out of logs that some of the Indians lived in, and there were very few. "I remember the first white person that I'd ever seen, scared me and my family half to death. We thought they were sick."

"I don't understand. You are white, just like us."

"I know, I know, but you have to understand, they were big like you, and all covered with hair and fur and stinky. Wow, did they smell. You could smell them coming a mile away, long before you ever heard them. Also, they talked like we are talking now, and at the time, my people couldn't understand them. It wasn't until much later that we could talk your language. I think you call it English."

"What language did you speak?" He said that there was no name for it, and that I could never understand it because it is spoken very fast. It dawned on me that it was probably the buzzing I had heard. I asked him to say something in his own language, and when he did, it was just a fast, buzzing sound. His lips were just a blur. I laughed, and he gave me a funny look. I said that I had heard it before, and now I understood what it was.

"Anyway, back to the stinky ones—that's what we called them. They were like a bunch of scared cattle; they ran or hid from everything they didn't understand. My father tried to talk to some of them one time, and they ran away, scattering all over a hillside, screaming. One of them tried to shoot my dad with a gun, and so a vote was taken by the elders whether a few darts and arrows should be stuck in them. The elders decided that we could hurt and harass them a little, but not kill them."

"Well, I'm glad that didn't happen. What finally did happen?" John said that some of the younger people covered their bodies with white dust and chased a bunch of the stinky ones all over the country until they got tired of laughing and of hearing the stinky ones scream. He said that he had heard that some of the Indians told them not to be scared of us.

"Anyway, things calmed down, but my people still wouldn't trust or have anything to do with them. Although the stinky ones almost starved during the winter, so my people would chase animals to them without them knowing about it."

A light went on in my head. I said "My God, was this up north by the Columbia River, close to the ocean?"

John gave me a funny look. "Yes, why?" Good grief, I just about fell out of my chair.

I started laughing and said, "Come over here with me," and I took John over to the other side of the front room and asked him if he recognized the picture on the wall. My wife had given me that picture of William Clark and Meriwether Lewis for Xmas.

John looked close at the picture but couldn't recognize them. He turned to me and said, "Wayne, the stinky ones didn't look clean like this picture, and that was a long time ago." I told him that Lewis and Clark were the leaders of a group of people that came across the United States during the early eighteen hundreds and built and stayed in a fort up around the Columbia River. John started to laugh, saying that it was probably them, but it wasn't much of a fort. He said they built some log huts because they were scared of his people. He said that they stayed there for about a year and then went back to where they came from. His family didn't think that they would see any more white big people again. Boy, was that a mistake.

John said that these were the first of my people that he had ever seen, but there were legends of them being around long, long before. I asked him to tell me some of the legends and just how long his people had been here in this area. He just looked at me and grinned and then said, "OK, I have time to tell a few." Meanwhile, I got up and filled his glass again.

John was a little evasive about some things. I got the feeling he wasn't telling me everything. I couldn't fathom the reason at the time, but I found out later. Wow, another surprise. But I don't want to get into that now.

John started telling me about some of the history and legends of his people. The little people do not have a written history; it's all word of mouth, passed down generation after generation. Now, don't get me wrong, I'm not suggesting that it is inaccurate. They might embellish it a bit to serve their immediate purpose, but as a whole, it is quite thorough. John, I might add, is a master storyteller—or, as I found out later, keeper of the legends, as the little people call him.

I came to understand that the little people had come to this continent about the same time as our people, but long before our history books tell of it. In fact, a long, long time before Columbus. It's not real clear to me where they came from, but I think from Europe, somewhere around Ireland. John did say that there were no people living in this country at the time, but there were some very big and nasty creatures. I think the little people, along with our people, got here by boat, but John didn't get into it too much. I did get the impression that they came together. But our people, the big people, didn't know about it. The little people must have stowed away on their boats. Apparently, the little people helped our people during the bad times, but most of our people were not aware of that either.

Actually, I think the little people have been helping our people from day one, but few of our people know about it.

John went on to say that other people showed up in this country, but much later, and that they eventually merged with the big people that were here. I stopped John at that time and asked, "Do you mean to tell me that the Indians, or brown skins, as you call them, are a mix of my people and some other race of people from a different continent?"

John said, "Yup, but I don't know whether they were your people. But big white people anyway." He said that later, about five or six hundred years ago, a bunch of white big people arrived on the other side of the country by boat and thought they had discovered the whole country. They were all fools and would have all died if it hadn't been for his people and the brown skins.

I stopped John about this time and asked him a question that I had been dying to ask. "John...do the little people believe in a God like we do? Or in something else?"

John just sat there and gave me a stupid look like I was an idiot and said, "For gosh sake, of course we believe in God." But their belief was a little different than ours. They believed that God had a lot more to do with nature, with a little magic thrown in. He said that if it's one thing his people liked and enjoyed, it was any-thing to do with magic. I had already had that impression from just being around them.

John told me that his family moved into the area where they live now about a hundred years ago. Before that, they lived farther up the valley, toward our city of Portland.

All the time John was in my house, about two hours, long enough to finish the bottle of scotch and get pretty tipsy, he seemed to talk in kind of a guarded manner. He chose his words pretty carefully. He did let a few things slip at the last though. The reason I know is that he would cuss when he did. I thought I would have to make sure I had another bottle when John came back.

When John was leaving, he stumbled down the porch steps, saying good-bye and that he would be back because he had a lot more to say. I thought that if he took off fast like the little people usually do, he was going to crash into a tree or something. But he didn't. I could hear him thrashing through the brush behind the house and cussing. I think John really enjoyed cussing, although he never used the Lord's name in vain. He did use some phrases that I had never heard though.

CHAPTER 14

I saw various members of the little people through the next year; they always popped up when not expected. They seemed to be waiting for something, and I finally found out what it was. They were worried about the land being for sale, the land they lived on.

Every time Jamie saw me, he would ask if I had heard anything. They never said it, but I got the impression they were going to leave the area if and when the land sold. Jamie had told me previously that this whole area had once been a large forest; that's what it was like when they first moved here. Now that little area was all that was left. The little people prefer to live in and around oak forests. They live mainly by hunting and eating small animals and birds that live in the forests, and the forest gives them protection from predators like the eagles. There are not many large oak forests left in the Willamette Valley. Most are small patches here and there, like the one Jamie's family lived in. The farmers need all the tillable land they can use to grow crops, so consequently, there go the forests and the wildlife habitat.

I had told Jamie that I had put up for sale some property that Linda and I owned on the Oregon coast, and that as soon as it sold, I would try to buy the land where he lived. I had already discussed it with the real estate agent who had it listed, and he had said he would ask the owner if he would split off the land that I wanted when I sold my property. Hopefully they wouldn't sell their property before we sold ours.

During the first year that the farmer had the land up for sale, I never saw anyone come to look at it. But the second year, after we expressed interest in buying it, I saw a number of people walking around on the property. Every time I saw someone walking toward the woods where the little people lived, I would go out and try to lead them in a different direction. I don't know why I worried about it. Heck, I had walked through those woods a number of times before I met the little people, and I never saw anything. There is no doubt that the only time a person is going to see them or their homes are when they want them to. It was probably something magical, like John brought up but wouldn't tell me much about.

Jamie appeared in front of me one day. He told me that he had seen the agent showing a person around the property. He said he didn't like him. I asked, "Who? The agent or the client?

He said both. "I had one of them twist his ankle and the other bonk his head while he was walking under a leaning tree."

"Good grief, Jamie, don't do that. That's not going to help matters." He said that he could have and wanted to do a lot worse, but his wife wouldn't let him. He said that they both looked and sounded like crooks to him, and he wanted to shoot an arrow in both of them. I laughed, but he didn't, and I thought, *My God, he's serious.*

I told him not to worry about it too much yet. I said that even if they did sell the property, the new owners might not cut down the forest. He said, "Ha; big people have been cutting down the trees since they came here." He added that it was a wonder that there were any trees left anyway in the whole valley. I couldn't really argue with that point.

Jamie was not in a very good mood, so I thought it would be better to go on my way. If there's one thing I've learned since I met the little people, it's that if they are angry or in a mischievous mood, it's best to get away from them in a hurry because someone is going to pay. And I didn't want that someone to be me. I know that in the past, after I had a disagreement with Sara or even Darcy. And that I had some strange things happen to me. One time while I was working in the garden, I got a burning and itching feeling in places that I don't want to mention and had to run into the house to take a shower. I just figured I had got something on myself from the plants when I relieved myself behind the barn. Anyway, when I came back out of the house, Darcy and some of her friends were there giggling, so I figured she had something to do with it. I didn't confront her with it because of the private spot it involved, but I just know I was at the wrong end of a joke. Actually, if I remember right, Darcy was mad at me for something at the time, but I don't remember what I was.

Anyway, I went back to what I was doing, and Jamie left. He seemed pretty disturbed, and I couldn't blame him. I sure hoped Linda and I could sell our property in time and the farmer would sell us the land that Jamie's family lived on. Actually, I wished I had enough money to buy the whole piece that was for sale, but that wouldn't happen. They wanted way too much, and I could never come up with that.

CHAPTER 15

One day in the spring—the other property was still for sale—I noticed Bruno was all upset about something. He kept whinnying and barking at the back gate. I figured someone was back behind the house, so I decided to go back there and tell them that the land was posted and to leave. I walked a little ways across the field to where the creek ran through some brush and a small stand of trees. There had been a few deer hanging around there, and I thought Bruno might have been able to smell them and maybe that was what he was barking at.

It was a beautiful warm day, not a cloud in the sky. I was wearing only a tee shirt and Levi's, and I started to sweat before I got across the field. I had almost got to the creek when I heard a noise in front of me, so I got down on my hands and knees and crawled around a bush to see. Good grief. I just froze. There was Darcy and five or so other young girl friends of hers, swimming in a small pool of the creek. A couple of the girls weren't swimming but running around in the grass, and they were all giggling and having a good time, having fun like all young people do. Except for one thing: none of them had a stitch of clothes on.

I immediately dropped down under the bush, out of sight. Then I thought, as I was lying there, that it was a stupid thing to do. *Now if they see me, they'll think that I am spying on them.* I must have stayed there for five or six minutes, trying to figure out how I could sneak back out of there without being seen, when a little voice, right beside me, said, "Are you enjoying yourself, Wayne?" My God, I could have wet my pants.

I slowly turned, and there was Sara standing beside me, looking around the bush, trying to see what I was looking at.

I said, "Damn it, Sara, you scared me to death, I didn't hear you come up." Then I decided the best thing to do was to tell the truth, so I explained to her what had happened. I said that I was so sorry, that I knew what it looked like, but I really didn't mean to be looking at the girls.

She gave me a funny look and asked, "Why?"

"Why what?"

"Why are you sorry that you are looking at the girls?"

I kinda stuttered a little and said, "Because they're skinny-dipping."

"They're what?"

"You know, swimming without anything on: naked."

Sara just stood there and looked at me. "Wayne," she said, "is something wrong with you this morning? The girls are here at the creek, taking a bath and washing themselves, just like I came to do." As she was saying this, she proceeded to take her clothes off.

I turned redder by the second. I might add, that's about all the time it took for Sara to get completely undressed and stand in front of me stark naked with a silly smile on her face. Remember, I was sitting down, not standing up, and Sara was standing right in front of me. Good grief, I was embarrassed to death. I think I've mentioned before that these may be little people, only two or three feet tall, but they are built and look just like us, and here was this beautiful, fully mature woman standing in front of me without any clothes on. I might be on the old side, but not that old. Without saying another word, up and out of there I went, straight across the field to home.

I went into the house, washed my face, and made a cup of tea. While drinking the tea, I heard a noise outside. The dogs were running around barking, so I got up and went to the door. Jamie, Sara, and Darcy were in the backyard playing with Bruno and Mercy. I went outside and tried to be social, but I was still a little flustered over what had happened earlier.

They all acted like nothing had happened. Jamie said that Darcy had something to say to me.

Darcy couldn't look me in the eye as she said she was sorry for playing a trick on me. I asked, "What trick?" She explained that she and the girls knew I was working outside alone and that if they made enough noise, I would come to investigate. They also knew how I would react to the girls taking a bath, and they thought it would be fun to see my reaction. I guess I should have realized that nobody would ever have seen them, let alone seen them taking a bath, unless they wanted them to. She said that they hadn't planned on her mother coming along.

I looked over at Sara, and she was looking off into the trees, acting like she wasn't paying attention or listening. I had a funny feeling that Sara knew what was going on, that she hadn't appeared beside me, behind that bush, out of happenstance. I think Jamie knew about it too because he just stood there grinning at me.

I've said it before, and I'll say it again. The little people just love to play practical jokes on people, themselves included. I guess I should feel lucky; at least I didn't get shot in the fanny or some other place with a dart or arrow.

Darcy signaled with her finger for me to bend down and kissed me on the cheek. She then whispered in my ear. "Wayne, I would never do anything to hurt you. You know that. I owe you my life, and that's a very important thing to me. Please don't be mad. I will never tease or pull a joke on you again, I promise, and I won't let any of my friends, either." I told her it was OK and not to worry about it. She said good-bye and left.

Jamie asked, "You aren't mad, are you?"

I answered, "Of course not. I know that you people don't know any other big people beside me, so I guess that I'm the one elected to suffer from some of your little games now and then." My God, you would have thought that I had just said the funniest joke in the world. Jamie and Sara, both, were rolling around on the ground, laughing so hard they had tears rolling down their faces. Of course, that got me laughing too.

When Jamie finally calmed down a little bit, at least enough to talk, he said to come over to their home in a couple of hours, that they had something to show me. He wouldn't tell me what the surprise was. I figured it was another practical joke, but he assured me that it wasn't. He did say that it was something that I would really like—all big people did.

CHAPTER 16

Later on that afternoon, I was sitting in the house reading a book, when I remembered what Jamie had said about coming over to their place. As I left, I got attacked by Bruno and Mercy, who thought we were going for our afternoon walk. So I decided to take them across the field to Jamie's.

I received a little different welcome this time. It seemed that some of the people, most of the people, were happy to see me, but some were not. I didn't understand why, so I approached Sara, who was standing and talking with a bunch of women. They seemed to be in a semi-heated discussion about something, and I was reluctant to intrude. Lord knows what would have happened to me if I insulted them by unintentionally interrupting.

Sara noticed me and came stomping over. I asked if there was something wrong. She just stood there for a couple of seconds, staring up at me like women of all ages and sizes can do, making men feel like total idiots. Finally, she said that some of the people didn't want Jamie to show me the things that he was going to. I told her that I didn't know what she was talking about in the first place, and in the second place, if some of the little people didn't want me there, I was going home. And at that, I immediately turned around and headed back the way I came.

She ran up behind me and grabbed the lower back of my coat and said, "I wouldn't do that if I were you." I must admit that I stopped right fast because that sounded like a warning, and I had no intention of getting Sara mad at me. She said, "Wayne, Jamie is doing this all for you, so just calm down and see it through."

"Sara, I have no idea what you are talking about. Jamie just asked me to come over here this afternoon. He never gave a reason, and I thought it was just an invite to visit."

Sara looked at me for a minute and then just started laughing. "Wayne, Jamie is going to show you one of the biggest secrets of our people. Something no other big person knows about or has ever known about."

"Good grief, I don't want to know anything like that. What if I accidentally told someone else? What would you do to me, bury me or shoot me with a dart, or something worse?" She just stood there and grinned at me, sending chills up my spine. I started to wish that I had never found that pipe a couple of years ago.

Jamie came over to us with a grin on his face. He said, "Well, I finally got it OK'd with most of the older men." He turned to Sara and asked, "How did you do?"

Sara answered, "Well, most of the women are pretty hesitant but agreed only because it was Wayne, who had already risked his life for one of our people, and they all felt a strong attraction to him." I just stood there blushing like an idiot with both of them grinning at me and having absolutely no idea what they were talking about.

Jamie, looking up at me, said, "Wayne, do you remember that gold powder that you have seen Sara use on injuries? You know, the stuff that saved your life and Darcy's life during the eagle attack."

"Of course I remember it. I figured it was a magical potion you little people have that cures anything."

Both Jamie and Sara started laughing. Jamie said, "Well, it is a little magical, I guess," looking over at Sara, who gave him a wink. Jamie went on to say that the people's healers, like Sara, do add their own ingredients to it, but the main part of it comes from the ground and has been around since the dawn of time. Jamie said that the substance is a mineral that is really quite plentiful but sometimes hard to find, and that some of the young people had just brought in some the previous day. He asked me if I would like to see it before the people started to process it into powder.

I didn't really understand why he thought that I would want to see it. Sometimes I'm a little dense, and since I felt a little like I was intruding that morning, I really wanted to just go back home. I finally understood when Jamie took me around the corner of one of the little buildings, and I just about fell over.

The sun was shining through the trees right on the biggest pile of what looked like gold that I had ever seen or even heard about. It was brilliant, reflecting the light in all directions because the pile consisted of all-gold rocks or nuggets. I was speechless. Now, I have seen gold before; maybe never that much, but I have seen pictures of gold bricks in *National Geographic Magazine*, and I saw small gold nuggets when I lived in Alaska, and I've seen it in jewelry shops, but I had never seen anything like I was looking at right then. My gosh, it was just beautiful, that is all I can really say. Jamie and Sara were standing in some of the reflected light, and it looked like they were glowing. How I wished that I had a camera with me so I could take a picture of them. Actually, they weren't looking at the gold; they were watching me and my expression.

They were both smiling when I asked, "Is that what I think it is?" Jamie said yes, it was gold. He went on to tell me what it came from.

He said that the younger ones of their people search for it all the time. They have ways to find it that they keep to themselves. When they do find some, they bring it back to the village, and then it is stored and hidden until some ointment has to be replenished. Then it is brought out and processed by their healers. He said that it has to be in a pure form, like we were looking at; it could have no impurities mixed with it because if it was heated to separate it from other minerals, that would make it useless for what they used it for. I could definitely tell that what I was looking at was pure.

Jamie leaned over and picked up a small nugget and handed to me. It felt warm in my hand. Not only did it make my hand warm, I started to feel warm and tingle all over, and I almost dropped it. It was not a bad feeling at all, and I noticed that my hand and exposed arm was starting to kind of glow. I wasn't worried and felt a peaceful like feeling coming over me. I looked over at Jamie and Sara. They were still smiling and still had that glow to them. Then it dawned on me that being close to the gold was making them glow just like me, not the sun reflecting off of it.

My face must have had a look of wonder on it because Sara said, "Don't be worried, Wayne. You are a little like us now. Let me explain. When I healed you by using our healing powder that is made basically from what you are looking at and holding, I changed you a little in a way that I cannot really explain. From now on, for the rest of your life, your body will react this way when you touch or get close to pure gold. Now you know one of the ways our young people find it. They start getting the feeling that you feel right now, any time they get close to it."

Sara said that she was sorry that she had kept this information from me. She said she had had no choice. She had to use the medicine when the eagle attacked me, or I would have died, and the elders would not let her tell me until now.

I asked what finally changed their minds, and Jamie said that he did. He had told them that my wife Linda worked in a jewelry store and that sooner or later, I would come into contact with pure gold that had not been processed and that our doctors would probably think it was some kind of allergic reaction. He told them that it would be better to forewarn me first.

Jamie and Sara could probably tell by the look on my face that the information was definitely a surprise and not going over too well. I really did not know what to think. I mean, don't get me wrong, I really appreciated what Sara did for me. It's just that I felt changed, or something like that. Then I remembered a funny feeling I'd got a while back when I put on a watch I owned that had some gold nuggets attached to it. It was a warm like feeling in my wrist. I had decided not to wear it at the time, and I hadn't put it on since.

Apparently, I was going to be like this the rest of my life, according to what Sara was telling me. I wondered what changes, if any, it had on the rest of my body, and I asked Sara about such. She looked at Jamie, and then looked around to see if anyone else was listening. Then, in a quiet voice, she said that there might be some other effects I probably should know about. She paused, and I said, not too nicely, "Go ahead, tell me."

Sara explained that no one, to her knowledge, had used the powder on a big person in her lifetime, so the total long-term effect was really unknown, but she did have a suspicion that my longevity might be more like theirs than a big person's anymore. I just looked at her and said, "Say again?" She said that I might live to be two hundred years old, like them, instead of the normal big-person lifetime. Lord, I just about fell over.

I decided that I wanted to go home, right then, and think about this. I abruptly turned around and headed in that direction as Jamie and Sara told me to come back. I just waved over my shoulder and kept on going. On the way back to the house, all I could think about was the fact that I did not—and I repeat, not—want to outlive my family and friends.

I'm not much of a drinking man, but when I got home, I put some 7UP in a glass and then added a whole bunch of whisky. I then sat down in my chair and drank it, meanwhile thinking the whole thing over and deciding that I was a real butt for walking out on Jamie and Sara after all the trouble they went through to get permission to tell me what they had. Just about the time that I decided to get up and wobble over to Sara and Jamie's, I heard a small knock on the back door.

I got up and answered it, and guess who? It was Jamie, and he didn't look too happy. I immediately said that I was sorry for leaving so suddenly. That I was having a hard time digesting what Sara had told me. He looked at me for a couple seconds and then down at his feet. He said, "Yeh, I probably would have felt the same way." I asked him if he would tell Sara that I was very sorry for acting the way I did and that I would make it up to her.

I immediately heard the word, "How?" from behind me, startling me, and I about fell off of the back step. I caught myself on the handrail and turned, seeing Sara. "Damn, Sara, if you don't quit doing that..."

She looked at me for a second and laughed. "Wayne, you are drunk."

"Just a little, maybe."

Anyway, Sara graciously agreed to ask some of the elders from the other families if anyone was aware of the ramifications of using their medicines on big people.

She came back over about a week later and let me know what she found out. It wasn't much because the little people just didn't have contact with big people like me. She did make a point of telling me that I could still die in an accident or from a bad disease, if that's what I wanted so badly. I got the impression that she thought I was acting a little foolish. Maybe she was right, I don't know. But it just didn't sit right with me.

CHAPTER 17

We had a hot tub in the back of the house in kind of a built-on gazebo. It was totally out of sight of the road, so nobody could possibly see when we were using it...or so I thought.

One evening, Linda and I were in the tub. It was after dark, and neither one of us had any clothes on, which was common for us when we were alone. We had been there for fifteen or twenty minutes when Linda decided that she had been in long enough and got out. She had just gone into the house and closed the door when I heard a giggle. I looked up, and on an oak tree limb about twenty feet away, there sat about ten or twelve little people men all in a row, passing around a jug of their homemade hooch.

When they found out that I had spotted them, you would have thought that was the funniest thing in the world. They were laughing so hard, two of them fell off the limb into a bush and were still laughing when they hit the ground. Of course, I got mad. I can't stand peeping toms no matter how small they are, and I told them so. I also told them to get down out of that tree and get out of here, using different words that I won't mention, of course. You wouldn't believe the commotion they made getting down and leaving. I really don't know how to describe it—little people falling everywhere, giggling, screaming, yelling, and I even heard one of them pass gas real loud, and that really made everyone laugh, including me. How could I possibly stay mad?

Then they all came over to me and handed me the jug of hooch, which I took a big swig of. I recognized most of the little people, including Jamie and John, his great-grandfather. In fact, I took one more drink, then handed the jug to John. Then I picked up Jamie and threw him in the hot tub, clothes and all. That did it. In a blink of an eye, every little person there was in the hot tub, some with and some without clothes. As I've said before, nudity means nothing to little people—and, I might add, a couple of the men weren't men, but little old ladies. I'll tell you! That was the biggest commotion that you could imagine in your wildest dreams. I just sat down, bare-ass nude, on the floor and laughed, and laughed, and laughed.

Why Linda didn't hear the noise and come back out, I couldn't understand. Then, probably because of the hooch, I decided this would be the perfect time for her to meet the little people and I yelled, "Linda, come here a minute!" Well now, you would have thought a bomb went off. Everything moved so fast, I couldn't really see it, and by the time Linda stuck her head out the door and asked what I wanted, it was dead quiet and all the little people were gone. I asked what she was doing—didn't she hear anything?

She informed me that she had and still was on the phone to her mom. Then, on second thought, she turned back to me and asked, "Hear what?" Before I could answer, she asked, "What is all that water doing on the floor, and what are you doing sitting out there?" I answered that I had stubbed my toe. She went back into the house. I started to clean things up and put the cover back on the hot tub.

I had just finished when I heard a little voice. "Wayne..." I turned around, and there was Jamie, totally soaked and dripping. I asked why he hadn't changed clothes and said that he was probably going to get sick from something. He said that he had gone home, but Sara kicked him out when she found out how he got wet. She made him come back over to see if I was mad. He added, "She was pretty upset that I got her floor wet too." He looked sheepish at me and asked, "Are you mad?"

"No, not really. I was just surprised to see you up in that tree." I told him how lucky he was that Linda didn't see him; she would probably have gone for her shotgun.

His eyes got real big, and he asked "Why?"

"Jamie, there are a few things that are different between your people and mine, and one is nudity. Linda would not—and I mean *not*—take it kindly to find out that a group of men, no matter how big they were, was watching her naked in our hot tub." I added, "Personally, I don't like the idea of someone watching me either."

About that time, I heard a little pop, and there was Sara, standing beside Jamie. She asked, "Did you tell him everything" He said that he was going to but he hadn't got to it yet.

I had a queer feeling, and I just looked at Jamie and asked, "There's more?"

OK, Jamie started jabbering, and the gist of whole thing was that this was not the first time they had watched Linda and me get in the hot tub nude. In fact, it was kind of a common occurrence. Now, if that wasn't bad enough, apparently they used to take bets on when would I get romantic with Linda. Good grief, you could have knocked me over with a feather. I just stood there for a minute with my mouth open, and then I asked, "Why, for God's sake, would you do that?" Jamie's explanation was that his people loved to wager, and they would bet on just about anything. I could believe that. He said that it had started long before we'd got acquainted and that my house was not the only one they visited now and then. That the people never knew that they were there, usually. They got lax around our place because they knew me.

He said, "What's the difference? You watched our girls taking a bath and swimming in the creek a while back, and you tried to stay hid." I just looked at Sara, and she just stood there with a big grin.

I came back with something like, "That was an accident, I didn't mean to be there, and I was hiding so the girls didn't think I was watching them."

Everything went quiet. We just stood there looking at each other, and I thought, *Oh crap, who really cares about this anyway* and said something stupid, implying that those little girls were cute, but I didn't consider myself cute, lying around naked in a hot tub. With that statement, of course, Jamie and Sara hit the floor in fits of laughter.

Sara had always wanted to look inside our house and see how big people lived, so I invited them to bring their family over in a couple of days. Linda had to go out of town to a sales managers' meeting for two days, and since I really didn't have anything to do that time of year, I figured I would get it over with.

Anyway, two days later, I was lying in bed asleep around seven o'clock in the morning when all heck broke loose. I couldn't figure out what was going on. I finally got awake and found that there were four or five little people on top of me, grabbing my hair and trying to kiss me. I tried to push them aside and sat up. I looked around and saw about thirty little people in my bedroom, all giggling and laughing.

I recognized Darcy as one of the little girls trying to kiss me on the cheeks and said, "What in heaven's name are you kids doing?"

She said, "Aw, come on, Wayne, just lie there and enjoy it." That got the whole room of little people roaring. She added, "Mom said that we adopted you as one of our grandpas, so we are treating you like a grandpa." I happened to notice John across the room sitting in the only chair, with his hands around his stomach. He was smiling and laughing and having too much fun.

I asked Darcy, "Isn't John your great-grandpa?"

"Yes, of course."

"Why don't you girls go over there and show me how you treat a real grandpa?" John heard me, his eyes got big, he quit laughing, there was a loud pop, and he was gone—followed by five little pops, and the girls were gone. Then I got to laugh with everyone else who was left in the room.

All the little people left the room and closed the door so I could get up and get my clothes on. When I went out, they were all over the house—looking in the closets, looking at pictures and all of Linda's little pretties. They wanted me to turn the television on. I was reluctant after what had happened when John was there earlier, but I did, and nothing happened. I guess they were braver in numbers. They were totally fascinated with the TV...I showed Jamie how to change the channels with the remote. I explained that it was a picture, nothing was real. That the people and what they were looking at was a long ways away. All twenty-five or thirty little people sat right there on the floor in front of the television like a bunch of little kids and never said a word or moved. I thought, *My God, now they are going to have to meet Linda because they are going to be over here all the time.*

Darcy, the girls, and John popped back in. Actually, John popped in and right back out again; I guess he wasn't going to have any more of the television. Darcy and the girls were just like everyone else—totally taken over by it. They kept changing channels, looking at everything they could.

I thought I should feed them something because they were always giving me food at their place, but I didn't know what to get. I finally decided to cook pancakes with maple syrup. Good grief. I went through two boxes of pancake mix and two bottles of syrup. When they left, not only did they go home happy, they went home full. I heard some complaints of stomach aches as they went out the door.

Sara said she would be back with some of the women to clean up after they took care of the children. I was happy to hear that. I didn't know how I was going to get the house clean and back in order before Linda got home. Anyway, Sara was back in about five minutes with five other little women. Now, I want to tell you, I've never seen anything like that. Those little women had brooms, mops, and rags, and they just told me to stay out of the way. It was just a big blur, and they were done in about ten minutes. The house was spotless. Nothing was out of place. In fact, it was *too* clean. I knew I was going to have to throw some lounge pillows around and muss a few things up, or Linda was going to notice.

When they were done, Sara jumped up on the dining room table and told me to come over there. She gave me a hug and a kiss on the cheek and thanked me for the day. And then pop, they were all gone.

CHAPTER 18

Linda and I are deer hunters. I had never seen any of the little people while we were hunting around our property, but I'm sure they saw us and knew what we were doing.

The property around our place was posted with No Trespassing signs by the farmer who owned it, though he allowed us to hunt. He also gave permission to a few other local people who asked him. The trouble was that a lot of people didn't ask; they just went hunting or trespassing anyway, and these people were generally the ones that did damage to the property and have no concern for the hunting rules and regulations. I had bullet holes in my barn door to testify to the fact.

Anyway, one morning during deer season, I was taking the dogs for their early morning walk. We were about a quarter mile from the house, on the paved road. There were no cars parked along the road that I could see, so I thought that no one was around hunting. I would never take the dogs for a walk if I thought some-body was around my place carrying a gun.

We had just passed a timbered area and were com-ing up to a small field with another bunch of brush and timber on the other side. I heard a loud scream and saw a person run out of the brush and throw a rifle in the air and then start rolling around in the field. He was dressed in camouflage clothes, so there was no doubt he had snuck into the area without permission. Most hunt-ers with permission wore orange hats or vests.

It was quite a commotion: the man screaming, my dogs barking, and me trying to hold both big dogs from going out into the field—which, I might add, is no easy task.

After ten or fifteen seconds, the man jumped up and started running again. He came out of the field, crossed the road about fifty feet in front of me, and ran into another field. When he looked at me, he yelled, "You son of a b——!" That about floored me. What did *I* do? He ran on across that field and into some bush, out of sight.

I just stood there for a few minutes, trying to figure out what I had seen and why he had said that to me. I didn't recognize the man, of course; he was still some distance from me. I couldn't see the rifle that he had thrown into the air because it fell in the field, and the grass was too high. I decided not to go get it. I would probably get accused of stealing it or something.

While I was standing there getting my wits together, I heard some squeaking noises coming from the brush, and Bruno started barking again. It just started dawn-ing on me what I was hearing when I saw three or four little hands stick out of the brush and wave at me. I just started laughing. I knew then who was responsible for the man running and yelling. I just wondered who the little people were and what they had done.

When we had finished our walk and were almost back to the house, Bruno took off and of course ran right to Jamie, who was standing just inside of our driveway. Linda had gone to work, or he would never have been there. Before I got to him, I slightly yelled, "Was that you down the road in the brush?"

"No, but they came back and told me about it, so I thought I had better come over and tell you, since you saw it happen." I let him know that the only thing I saw was a man running and yelling. We both started laughing. I told him that it was kinda funny. The man was definitely not enjoying himself, but he wasn't getting hurt terribly bad, so I couldn't understand why he had blamed me, calling me "a son of a b——" when he ran by.

Jamie said that he didn't know why the man yelled at me. He did know why he was yelling and running though. Apparently, some little people kids were hunting birds when they came up on him sitting in the forest, waiting for a deer to walk by. They thought he had fallen asleep. Being the way kids are, they found a large hornet's nest and dropped it on his head. To make it worse, a couple of girls shot him in the bottom with their blowtubes when he ran by.

Now I was really laughing. I asked Jamie, "What's going to happen when the guy finds those blowgun darts in his fanny when he gets home?" He said that wouldn't happen because the darts were not hunting darts and didn't have barbs on them, and that they probably fell out as soon as he started to run. He added that the guy would probably get a small infection, though, because he thought the girls put something on the tips of the darts, something hot and stingy. I thought, *Oh my God, that's just awful*...even if the guy probably did deserve it. I didn't envy him at all.

I told Jamie that it appeared to me that all the kids spent most of their time just looking for mischief to get into, and it usually involved big people. We were both laughing. He said the kids were always playing pranks on everybody and everything, as I well knew, but they were not allowed to really hurt somebody or cause serious damage without permission from the clan council. The grown-ups couldn't either, and if anybody did, they were punished quite harshly.

We got off that subject and started talking about deer hunting. Jamie said that they didn't try to kill the big animals, like deer, very often. There was just too much meat to take care of unless they were going to have a big feast or clan gathering. He added, "We know that you and Linda hunt deer," and that the little people of his family might be able to help us if we wanted them to. "Of course, we might accept a piece of meat now and then." With that said, he grinned great big and started to chuckle. I just laughed out loud and waved over my shoulder as I walked the dogs back into the gate on our driveway.

Jamie was following me and still talking. He was saying, "You know, it doesn't have to be too big of a piece. We don't eat too much meat."

"I know. You'd prefer vegetables and fruit out of my garden, huh?"

Now, that got him laughing out loud. "Wayne, we really like the liver and heart. You and Linda don't care for those pieces of meat, do you?"

"Yes, of course we do." Then I noticed he was grinning at me, and it occurred to me what had happened the year before. I had shot a deer late in the evening, and I was in a hurry because Linda was working and I was by myself, and I wanted to get the deer back to the barn before it got dark. Anyway, I forgot and left the heart and liver where I had cleaned the deer and went back after dark with a flashlight to get it. Well, to my surprise, they were gone. I had just assumed that a dog or a coyote had got them. Now I knew different. I wasn't smiling anymore when I said, "Damn, Jamie, you could have at least told me." Jamie said that he thought that I had left them on purpose, since a lot of hunters do, and that he didn't know that I had come back to get them until a lot later. I still wasn't smiling, and I didn't say anything; I just looked at him. He looked down at the ground, acting kind of sheepish. I just grinned. I really didn't care; I was just giving him a hard time.

I finally said, "OK, Jamie, how are you going to help me and Linda hunt deer?" I added that I didn't want him or any of the little people around when we shot. It was too unsafe. I explained that we only shot the male deer with horns, and we were only allowed one deer apiece per year—although this year, we were allowed two apiece; we had special tags from the Game Commission.

Jamie began by saying, "Wayne, I have this all planned out." And I thought, *Gosh, here we go again.* I never really trusted anything any little person dreamed up because something always happened. Usually I was the one who suffered in the end. Well, Jamie explained how Linda and I should get up in our barn loft. That's a platform that I built in the roof of the barn that has a lid that can be lifted up. I also built a stairway up to the platform for easy access. When we stand on the platform, we can see all around our place, including into a big field behind our property, which is enclosed by forest land. Anyway, Jamie's plan was to have all the little people chase the deer out of the forest and into the field so we could shoot one. Now, this all sounded fine and dandy, except what if there were some other hunters in the forest? And I absolutely did not want any of his family in the field, out in the open. I expressed my concerns to Jamie and he just said, "Oh poof, don't worry about everything. We can take care of any hunters," and just stood there and grinned at me.

OK, the big day arrived. I thought the evening would be the best time because less chance of any other hunters around, and also Linda was working—which was a good thing because I didn't think a deer hunting episode was the time for Linda to meet Jamie and his family.

It was about four thirty in the afternoon. I had been sitting on a chair in the loft for about a half hour. I hadn't seen a deer. I knew that Jamie and his family were in the forests around the field because he came out and waved at me. Now, that about did it. I had almost made up my mind that I wasn't going to shoot if I did see a deer because of all the little people out there.

Well, I saw some brush move at the edge of the field, so I laid my gun down and reached down by my feet for the binoculars. When I stood back up, I was flabbergasted. The field was full of deer running in every direction. Now, I mean a lot of deer—probably at least twenty. Bucks, does, fawns, and some great big bucks; there were deer of all sizes. Now ask me if I was excited. I didn't know which one to shoot.

There was a big four-point on the left side of the field at about a hundred yards away. I thought about shooting at him, but that was the area where Jamie went into the brush. There was another huge buck, bigger than the one on the left, standing in the back of the field next to the brush line. He was about two hundred yards away, and there were three or four does standing all around him. I didn't want to take the chance of hitting one of them.

Then I noticed a nice buck coming up about fifty yards from where I was. He wasn't real big, just a forked-horn, but the size of his horns were unreal. That was probably the biggest forked-horn rack that I had ever seen, and I've hunted deer a long time—most of my life. I decided I was going to take that deer. He was out in the open, just below me, and I knew my bullet wouldn't carry into the brush or timberline. I shot once, he went down, and it was all over. I crawled down out of my loft in the barn, attached the trailer to the garden tractor, and drove around, into the field, and up to the deer.

I started to clean the deer when I heard somebody say, "Why didn't you shoot one of the big ones, Wayne?" I looked up and Jamie was standing right beside me. I answered that this deer was closer than all the rest, and I didn't want to shoot around the timber or brush where I thought he or his family might be. As I was telling him that this deer would also be better eating than one of the older ones, I noticed little people coming out into the field everywhere. They were all laughing and jumping around, like little people do.

I said, "Jamie, I thought just your family was coming."

"This is just my family." Then I remembered that the whole clan was his family. Most of them came up and stood around, watching me clean the deer. I had the heart and liver lying on the grass beside me, and I saw Jamie looking at them.

I said, "OK, you can have the heart, but I have to take the liver." I explained that Linda's mother was sick with a bad type of cancer, and she liked deer liver.

Sara was standing behind me, which I was not aware of, and she had to know all about it. I told her what I knew, which wasn't much, except that my mother-in-law was real sick. Sara said that the liver would be very good for her and anybody that was sick. She added that her own grandmother could sure use a little of it...she wasn't doing too well. Good grief, what was I to do? I said, "Why don't you take a little of it for her?" She replied that if it was all right with me, she would take the whole liver home and cut a little piece off for her grandmother and then bring the rest back to me later. I told her that would be just fine. I couldn't understand why she just didn't have me cut a little piece off of it right then and there, but I didn't say anything.

After I got the deer cleaned, Jamie's family helped me load it into the trailer. The deer was a little bigger than I'd thought; I was glad they were there to help. I saw Jamie all red in the face and huffing and puffing, and I grinned, saying, "Oh, you wanted me to shoot a bigger one, huh?" He just laughed. In fact, they all laughed.

I told Jamie that I was going to hang the deer up in the shop and that I would cut it up in three days. I added, "Come over then, and I will give you a couple of pieces."

CHAPTER 19

After I left Jamie and his family in the field, it was just getting dark when I got the deer hung up in the shop. I had brought it back, skinned it, washed it out, and then dried it out with towels. I had it hanging by its rear legs, and I was down on my knees trying to cut its head off with a meat saw when Sara popped up (literally). She had the liver in a little grass basket. She took it out and laid it on my bench, thanking me. She said her grandmother really appreciated it. I couldn't see where she had cut any off, and I told her so. She said she didn't need very much. I said that I would get up and put it in a ziplock bag and put it in the freezer.

She immediately said no. I looked at her with a question on my face. She added that the plastic bag would be all right, but not to put it in the freezer—to give the liver to Linda's mother, fresh, just the way it was, that it was better for her that way. Personally, I did not think it would make any difference, but I was tired, and I knew better than to question Sara about anything she told me to do. So I stayed on my knees and continued what I was doing.

She walked up, put her arm around my neck, kissed me on the cheek, and asked, "What are you doing?"

"Trying to saw this darn deer's head off," I answered. And added, "You're getting a little familiar, aren't you?"

She said, "Why, no...you are one of the family now, I can do whatever I want."

I stopped working and turned to her, saying, "Now, Sara, just remember, I'm a lot bigger that you are, and I am a very happily married man. And you are a very happily married woman." She jumped back with a funny look on her face, and I thought, *Boy, you've done it now.* I figured if it's one thing you don't do in this life, it's reject a woman, no matter what her size is, and especially being blunt the way I just was.

She looked at me for a few seconds and then just started laughing. She then threw both arms around my neck and gave me a great big, loud smooch on the cheek. "Boy," she said, "you men, no matter what your size"— and she emphasized the word *size*—"sure think you're cool, huh? A few hugs and kisses on the cheeks between friends is not some big, romantic episode." OK, now I was tired and getting to feel like a big fool. All I wanted to do was finish what I was doing and go in the house and sit down.

I did have a question in my mind about whether Sara did anything to or put anything on that liver, so I asked her. She just stood there and looked at me a few seconds and then asked, "What do you mean?"

"Sara, you told me that the gold stuff didn't work on diseases."

"You're right, it doesn't. But I did put some stuff on it that might help Linda's mother. It's the same medicine that I put on the piece for my grandmother. It sure can't hurt, and it might help her."

"What is it? Magic or something?"

"No...well, it might have a little." She grinned and said it was mostly natural ingredients that grow wild almost everywhere. She said, "Wayne, don't worry about it. I would not give anything to anyone in your family that would be harmful."

I asked, "Do you really think it's going to help someone with cancer, though?" I added, "By the way—do you know what cancer is? Do your people get cancer too?"

"Of course I know what the disease you call cancer is, and yes, we do get it, but not very often."

I bluntly asked, "Do you know how to cure it?" Sara just stood there for a couple seconds, not smiling, then held up her right hand, like waving good-bye, and pop, she was gone.

Now, I know the little people did not like to lie to me. They might not tell everything that I want to know about different things, but they very rarely tell me something that's not true. It didn't take a rocket scientist to figure out that Sara did not want tell me any more on that subject.

Well, I had told Jamie to come to the shop in three days. That's when I would cut up the deer and give them some. I don't think that was the thing to say. I had just cut a shoulder off of the hanging deer and laid it on my bench. I turned around, and there were twelve or so little people, all standing in a line, and each with one of those little grass baskets in his or her hand. All grinning, I might add.

I laughed and thought, *I should have shot that bigger deer, like Jamie said.* I turned to Jamie and said, "I thought everybody over there"—I indicated the forest where he lived—"cooked and ate out of a community pot..."

He answered, "Not all the time. And besides, we all have to contribute our share when we do."

They didn't really take that much. It took just a little more meat than was on that one shoulder to fill up their little baskets. Besides, you would have thought that I was giving them the biggest present in the world. Every one of them either shook my hand, hugged me, or kissed me on the cheek—some, all three. You just had to love the little people. My God, I have never seen a group of people in my life that was so affectionate or emotional. It kinda made me want to give them the whole deer, and I probably would have, but I knew they couldn't eat or keep that much meat.

Jamie said that they had eaten the heart the night before. They had cut it up into small pieces and put it in a stew, and they had eaten up the whole pot. I'll bet it was delicious. If it's one thing the little people can do, it's cook. I had quite a few meals over there, and I had never tasted anything that I didn't like. They seemed to really have a handle on the seasonings. I really didn't taste much salt or pepper, but the food didn't need it. It was always just excellent. I have tried a couple of times to watch the women cook, but the men or children are always around me or on me, and they are always filling my cup of their home brew. Now, let me tell you, when you start drinking their home brew, not too much else matters. That's probably the reason the food always tastes so good.

The day before I cut the deer up, Linda had a day off from work, so we drove over to her mother's house for a visit, and we took the deer liver to her. She did not look good at all. She was going through chemotherapy and wasn't doing very well with it. We didn't stay long. On the way back home, Linda got pretty upset. Neither one of us thought her mother was going to be with us too long; apparently the chemotherapy was affecting her heart. Linda wanted to take some time off of work to be with her mother. I told Linda she should call her in a couple of days and check on her.

Two days later when Linda got home, she drove into the carport, got out of the car, and said, "You are not going to believe this."

Standing close by, I said, "What?

"I just got off the cell phone with my mom. She said that she felt a lot better and that she had been up all day cleaning house." I just stood there and stared at Linda, and she stared at me.

I said, "My God, two days ago, she couldn't even hardly walk, let alone clean house."

Linda answered, "I know."

At the end of the week, Linda and I went back over to her mother's place and had the shock of our lives. Her mother looked great. She was running around in the house doing stuff and jabbering as always, and looked like she felt good. In fact, she said she felt wonderful. I looked at Linda and thought, *Oh my gosh, now she's going to have to call her sister and brother back and tell them the good news.* She had called them earlier and told them their mother wasn't doing well and that they had better come and see her.

Linda's mother turned to me and said, "I want to thank you kids for the deer liver." She said that she had cooked it the day we gave it to her and ate it up in two days. She said it was delicious, and she could feel it giving her energy the more of it she ate.

I was bent over petting her dog and not paying too much attention when she said that. When it dawned on me what she said, I just froze. I had forgotten all about that liver. In fact, we had got another deer since then, and I had it hanging up in the shed. Linda had gotten it on her day off. The liver and heart from that deer was sitting in a large bowl of water in the refrigerator. I hadn't planned on giving them to anybody; I was going to put them in the freezer. I thought, *I'm going to have a talk with Sara, whether she likes it or not.* I sure wasn't going to say anything to anybody else.

I straightened up, and Linda was looking right at me, staring me right in the face. I turned around real quick and started playing with the dog again. I didn't know if she was suspicious or not, but I knew something was on her mind. I'm not real good at keeping anything from my wife, but every time I'd brought up the little people, she gave me a bad time. She wasn't mean or mad or anything; she just laughed at me a lot and teased me, which was all right. I didn't care. I laughed right along with her. But this had something to do with her mother, and I wasn't real sure how she would handle that. I really didn't want to find out.

Linda's mother knew we had another deer; Linda had told her on the phone the day she got it. I said that I would save the liver for her. She was extremely happy to hear that. I thought that I was going to have to freeze it first, because I couldn't keep it fresh for another week until Linda's next day off, so I could take it over to Sara. I didn't know what Sara had done to the first one, except what she'd told me. I wasn't sure she would do it again if I asked, anyway.

A couple of days later, I was outside raking leaves, and Jamie popped up. (That is an excellent description of their appearances because that is exactly what they do.) He sat down on a rock and lit his pipe, so I knew he was in a visiting and talking mode, which was usually the case anyway. After he asked me about the weather and some other stuff that was stupid, I asked, "All right, Jamie, what's on your mind?"

He grinned at me a couple of seconds and then said, "Sara wanted to me to find out how Linda's mother liked that liver."

I replied, "Why? Why didn't Sara come and ask me?"

He got all flustered and said, "She just knew you were going ask her a whole bunch of questions that she couldn't answer." I thought, *Couldn't? Or wouldn't...*

I said, "Tell Sara that Linda's mother loved the liver and that she's doing fine. The liver really seemed to help her. Tell her that I don't know what she did to it, or even if she did anything to it—but just in case she did, that I really am grateful and I won't ask any more questions about it."

He got up to leave and then said, "Like I told you before, Wayne, there are some things that our wives and women know, especially the healers, that us men know nothing about. And we really don't want to know. Sara mentioned that you had asked her if we had a cure for a disease called cancer, the disease Linda's mother has, and that she didn't answer you. I really don't know myself, and I'm not real sure I know what cancer is because I have never known any of my people to have it."

I said, "Oh, heck, let's forget about it. It's no big deal," and I went back to work. Jamie left.

I thought, *I wonder what the little people die of. If they live to be two hundred years old, they have to die of something sooner or later.* I think most of the human race dies of disease, mainly cancer and heart disease or accidents. The only thing that I had heard of the little people dying from so far is eagles.

CHAPTER 20

Well, it finally happened. I was standing by the driveway when the real estate agent for the surrounding property drove up and told me that the property was sold, that a large farm corporation had bought it. I knew who he was talking about. I had met them earlier when they were out looking at the place. The people that I had talked to were pretty excited, so I knew they would try to get it.

Now, I knew there were two things that I had to do: tell Jamie and his family, and get a hold of the new owners to see if they would sell me some of the property behind my place where Jamie and his family lived.

Of course, Jamie did not take it too well. He jumped around, buzzed around, caused little whirlwinds, and just created a general ruckus like little people do when they get real, real mad. He stopped long enough to tell me, "Those farmers are not going to like working out here very much when we get through with them." I told him that would not help matters one bit.

He said that they would cut all the trees down so that he would have to move. I said to just wait and see, maybe they wouldn't. Although I knew he was right. I have never known a farmer yet that didn't try to spray and plow up everything possible, no matter what. I guess I couldn't really blame the farmers; it was just an investment to them, and they had to make money on it.

I told Jamie to just wait and see what would happen, that I was going to talk to them and would tell him what I found out. I told Linda that night when she came home. She said the same thing that Jamie said. She had been home when the farmers had looked at the property, and we had discussed it then. We were worried that they would cut all the trees down around our place, and we didn't like the idea of living out in the middle of a bunch of fields. I told her what I told Jamie: that I would talk to them and see what their plans were.

My chance came about two or three days later when I noticed a pickup parked in one of the fields. The vehicle was empty, but I found the guys in one of the patches of trees. It was the same two men that I had talked to earlier. Nice guys, I liked them both. I congratulated them on their purchase. I brought up the fact that I sure would be interested in buying some of the property behind my house. I got the impression from the older man that he thought that area was prime property and that they weren't real sure what they were going to do with it.

Later, I told Linda about running into the men again and the conversation that we had. I told her, "Honey, I think we'd better try and sell our place and move. I have a bad feeling about this." I had a distinct impression that they were going to change the whole area—cut the trees down, drain the wetlands, and put in new roads. I told her that I was afraid of what changes in the floodwater control might do to our property. It was fine now, but after they were finished, I wasn't sure what might happen. I did know one thing for sure: little property owners like us could not fight the big corporations and big landowners like them. It's amazing how big business and big money talks when it comes to getting permits and variances from different branches of the government. Linda totally understood.

I've mentioned that my wife doesn't adapt well to sudden changes and decisions. She has to think things out a little and make plans, talk ideas over, and so forth. Once plans are made, she's a ball of energy and enthusiasm, but until that time, it's a little slow going. I knew it wouldn't be easy for her, but eventually it would all work out fine.

Jamie and his family, on the other hand, might be another story. I wasn't real sure how to go about telling them about what I found out and my fears of what might happen. It might be like setting a bomb off (or at least a whole bunch of little bombs). Or, they might just leave the area gracefully. I really didn't believe the latter.

I ran into Darcy a couple of days later—or, should I say, she popped up, which is more like it. Anyway, I told her to tell her parents that I would bring Bruno and come over to see them that evening and that I had something to talk to them about. She looked around with a grim look on her face and asked, "Is it about the people who bought the property?" I absolutely did not like the way she asked that. And she had her little blowgun in her hand, and her knuckles were white from gripping it so hard. I thought, *OK, here it goes...there is no doubt going to be some misery in the lives of the people who bought that property*. I answered yes, but I wanted to see her family anyway, since I hadn't been over in quite a while.

When I crawled into the little people's living area that evening, you could have heard a pin drop. Everyone was sitting around with very unpleasant looks on their faces. At first I tried to be happy and laugh and talk to everybody, but it didn't work very well. Even the kids hardly played with Bruno. They just stood around and petted him. I thought that I had to change my plan of attack; this was not working out too well. So when I saw Jamie's grandfather, I told him that he had better get us a couple of cups of that home brew of his and that I thought we were going to need it. At least that brought a grin to his face.

I took a couple of drinks and told everybody to gather around. I thought that I might as well get right to it. I turned to Jamie and asked how hard it would be to move his family from here. He just looked at me, so I went on and told them everything that I knew about the farmers and their plans. I added, "I really don't think that life is going to be the same around this area at all.

Linda and I are planning on putting our place up for sale and moving."

Jamie explained that it wasn't that hard to move. The problem was finding a place to move to. He said, "Don't you remember? I told you about how our clan has lived in this certain area, and that no other family comes into our area except to visit or travel through." He said that it was going to be extremely hard to find another area that wasn't already occupied by another family. He said, "Don't you remember, Wayne? I told you I never have been across the big river. In fact, I have not been out of our area in my whole life. Some of our family have, but I haven't."

Jamie then asked me where Linda and I were going to move. I answered that I didn't know, that we had children and grandchildren living on the coast, which he already knew about, but I didn't really want to move back there. I did say that it wouldn't be too far away though.

Jamie said that they could move down closer to the river, where there were still plenty of oak and fir trees. He went on to say that the reason it wasn't farmed yet was the high water in the winter, but they would have to contend with that too. He gave me the impression that some of the elders were going to visit some of the other families that lived in the general vicinity and see if any of them knew of an open area.

Jamie went on to tell me something that kind of surprised me. He said, "You know how we travel so fast when we want to?"

"Of course I know. It startles me almost every time you or someone in your family pops up in front of me." He said that it would be hard to do that in a new, strange area. He explained that one of the only reasons they were able to travel so fast is that the area they grew up in was imprinted in their minds. In other words, they were born with a familiarity of all the trails and obstacles in their area. It wasn't just their family; all the families or clans were like that. He said that years and years ago, he understood that it was not like that—his people roamed all over the world, and it was a very bad time full of turmoil and clan wars. He said that was long before his family's or clan's memories.

The way Jamie was talking, I was beginning to understand that when his family was out of their area, they could not travel as fast—or at least, they could only for very short distances. This made them more vulnerable to predators such as cats and eagles. I was beginning to understand the little people's evolution over the millennia, and it was sure different from ours. I really did not know that much about the little people. I sure wished they had a recorded history. I knew I was really privileged to know of their existence, let alone anything more. I had been told by various members of the family that there had been contact with big humans like me in previous times, and usually it didn't turn out well. I just wondered if in any of these cases, somebody didn't record something about the history of the little people. I don't mean recently, but way back in time. I thought that when I had time, I was going to start checking old records and such to see what I could find out. I never really could understand why, if there were a lot of little people in the world, it wasn't common knowledge among my people. I mean, come on. People—or any animal, for that matter—leave evidence of their existence. My gosh, look at all the garbage our people leave everywhere.

I did ask Jamie what happened to his people after they died. I had never heard of little-people skeletons ever being found anywhere, or anything found that might indicate another race of people might be living among us. Lord a-mighty, I couldn't imagine what the newspapers would do with that information. Then, on the other hand, there are supposed to be sasquatches or bigfoots running around in our mountains, and I had never heard any real evidence, such as skeletons or the like, being found to prove that either.

Jamie did tell me that I probably never would see a little-person skeleton. That he never had. He had seen a drawing of one somewhere. He explained that it might look as if we were alike and just that his people were smaller; but as he had told me before, our bones were different. He said that when someone died, they didn't bury them like we do. They cover them with a clothlike substance, lay them on a low platform or table, have a ceremony similar to ours, and within a day, the remains have totally dissolved. The only thing that is left is the cloth and table. He said that you can actually see the body kind of shrink up, turn to dust, and blow away. I thought, *How cool is that.* I never have really talked to any of the little people about religion. I have always wondered about it though. I know they have a pretty strong belief about something, and I know that it coincides with nature—or anyway, our thinking on nature. I'm sure someday I will find out. Jamie said that maybe someday, if I was really interested, I would probably be allowed to witness a ceremony. They don't call it a funeral or burial. I told him I appreciated it, but I hated things like that, and if it was one of his family, I just didn't think I could handle it.

I was sitting on the ground and looking down when I said that, and when I looked up, a whole bunch of little people were standing right next to me, touching me and then hugging me, some looking very sad. As I've said before, the little people have the warmest hearts and are the most emotional people that I have been around or have ever heard about. Needless to say, when they react like that, it always makes my eyes water, and that always makes everything worse. Then they *really* want to hug and touch me. Oh, well, enough said about that.

Jamie asked, "Wayne, you're worried about us, aren't you?"

"A little bit," I answered and tried to laugh, but it didn't come out too good, and everybody started to laugh. I asked the whole group of little people, "Has anybody here ever ridden in a one of our vehicles?" I noticed they were all shaking their heads no. "Would anybody like to?" Boy, I saw a lot of heads shaking no real fast, and some of them in the back even left. Now I could really laugh. Jamie and Sara were standing right beside me. I looked right at them and asked, "You guys aren't scared to go for a ride in my pickup with me, are you?"

They looked at each other, and Sara said, "No. But why? I don't think we would enjoy it very much."

I said, "You might be surprised." I asked two other people—I only wanted to take four—to meet me at my place after Linda went to work the next day, and we would take just a short drive. Then, if everything went all right, later we would cross over the river and maybe even go to the coast some other day.

All the little people were looking at each other and not saying a word, so I added, "I'll tell you what. If four of you show up tomorrow morning, we will go. If you don't, we won't. It's no big deal." I looked over at Jamie's grandfather and asked, "Is there any more of that home brew? My cup is empty." That did it. The whole mood of everyone there immediately changed to merriment. Little people were laughing and running around. I thought, *OK, the party begins.* I laughed.

CHAPTER 21

Well, the next day, I wished that I had not made my offer. Linda had gone to work; it was eight o'clock, and no little people had shown up yet. I was beginning to feel a little relieved because I was a worried about what might happen.

I remembered what had happened in our house when Jamie's grandfather had seen the television for the first time. I did not want that to happen while I was driving down the road in the pickup. Good grief.

When I had returned home the previous evening, I had started to regret making the offer. I think I had just been acting like a big man because I had a couple of cups of their home brew. In other words, I was not thinking with all my faculties, using my head.

I was sitting on the back steps of the house when pop, pop, and there were Jamie, Sara, Darcy, and Davey standing in front of me. None of them looked real happy, and Sara said no one else wanted to go, so they'd decided they would.

I made a comment that I thought some of the elders might want to take a ride, and Jamie said heavens no, they were the ones who were most adamant against it. He said, "They still remember the horses and cows on the roads when there were none of your people's vehicles. Our people don't like your vehicles much; they've caused a lot of misery. A lot of us have been hurt or killed on your roads by your vehicles."

I asked, "How could that happen? You travel so fast."

He said that was the problem. They had to travel fast when they crossed a road so they weren't seen, and sometimes the younger people didn't take enough precautions—and some of the older ones didn't either. As he said this, he looked over at Sara. Sara just looked at him. I had seen that look before, so I didn't inquire about it.

I said, "OK, if you're sure you want to do this, come on," and I started for the pickup that was parked in the driveway. No one moved but me. They all just stood there with big eyes and stared at the pickup.

And then Darcy grabbed Davey's hand and said, "Come on, brother," and started to follow me. Sara and Jamie didn't move.

I had a short-bed Dodge pickup that had front and back seats but no back doors; you had to fold the front seat forward to get in the back. Anyway, I opened the front passenger door and folded the seat forward so that they could get in. I figured that because of their size, it would be the safest place to put them. After all, I didn't want to get stopped by a policeman and try explaining how come they were not all in car seats for children. The back windows were tinted, so I figured they would not be seen, at least not very easily; I didn't plan on going into any towns or stopping anywhere.

Darcy jumped right up in there, and Davey got in too, but a lot slower. I told the kids to pile up some of my coats and sit on them if they wanted to so they could see out, but I could see they would rather stand up in the seat.

Jamie and Sara still just stood there looking at the pickup. I said, "Jamie, how many times have you seen me driving around in that pickup?"

"A lot."

"Haven't you ever wished that you were with me?" I asked.

He answered, "Well, yes, I guess sometimes. It would be easier than running. But I think I can go faster than your pickup."

"You probably can, but that's not the point. The point is that you can sit there and look outside at all the scenery and sights and don't have to worry about running into anything. I'll be driving."

He said, "Oh, all right," and started for the pickup.

Sara hadn't moved or said a word. I said, "You know, Linda drives her car to work almost every day and drives my vehicle too, and it doesn't scare her. She's only two or three feet taller than you." Boy that did it. Here came Sara with a snort. I chuckled to myself, but I didn't dare show it.

I told them to hop up in the back with the kids and added, "If I tell you to, I want you all to lie down and hide behind the front seat so nobody can see you, OK?" I said that there were a lot of reasons for that and I didn't want to explain them all right then.

OK, I got in, put my safety belt on, and started the vehicle. My God, a coat flew over my head, dust was flying. I heard a whole bunch of high-pitched squeaking or squealing, and I shut the engine off. One of them had their arms around my neck, choking me from behind; one was on the floor in front of the passenger seat with head up under the heater with little feet and butt sticking out, and I couldn't see any sign of the other two. I figured they must be under the back seat.

I just sat there for a few seconds and said, "All right, whoever has a hold of my neck can let go so I can breathe now." To my surprise, it was Davey.

Jamie stood up in front of the right passenger seat, and the two women got back up in the back seat.

I had an idea. I told the rest of them to crawl over the front seat and come up beside me, which they did. Then I showed them the ignition and how I started the vehicle and explained to them how noisy the engine was going to be and that it was not dangerous and yes, the vehicle was going to hum and vibrate.

When I got done talking, they kind of settled down a little, and a little color was coming back into their faces. Although I think if a door had been open, they would have been gone—and no, I hadn't shown them how to open a door yet.

Actually, I was starting to have a lot of fun with this.

OK, I tried again. I started the engine, and they all just stared at me in the face. I smiled and said, "See?

That's not so bad, huh?" None of them said a word. I let the engine run a little while so they could get used to it, and they did. They quit looking at me and started looking out the window.

I told them to all get in the back seat again, which they did. Then I sat there a little longer, explaining what I was going to do, like putting my foot on the brake, putting the vehicle in gear, and giving it some gas.

I then executed everything I told them, and we started to move. I felt little hands grabbing my sweatshirt from behind. I looked at the inside rearview mirror and saw a whole bunch of little faces and big eyes. I was really chuckling to myself, thinking they all probably deserved this for some of the little tricks and pranks they had pulled on me in the past.

I drove about three miles in a big circle and came back to our driveway. I then drove behind the house, stopped the vehicle, shut off the engine, and said, "How was that? Did you like it?" No one had said a word since we had left, but they sure did then.

My God, they were all jabbering at once, saying that there was nothing to it, and that was a piece of cake, and it was really fun, and so forth. I said, "Good, I'm glad you really enjoyed it. Because we are leaving again and going further this time." Having said that, I started the engine again.

They just froze, not saying a word and staring at me, then looking out the window as we started to move again. We were going by some oak trees and I heard Davey say, "I got a big squirrel in there one time, remember, Dad?" That did it; Davey had broken the ice, so to speak. All of them started talking at once and pointing out things as we drove by.

I must have gone about six or seven miles, staying away from any small towns, and hadn't met a car yet. But when I did, the proverbial stuff hit the fan.

We were only traveling about forty miles an hour, and so was the car meeting us. I saw it coming and thought, *Oh, Lord, I forgot to explain about this happening.* It was about a hundred feet away and had just come out of a corner—that's why I didn't see it earlier. The little people in the back seat saw it the same time that I did and were immediately silent.

I had just got "It's OK" out of my mouth when they all reacted like they had at the first. This time they all went under the back seat and screamed. My gosh, I just about soiled my sweatpants. I have mentioned before how piercingly they can scream when they feel they are in danger; well, there were four of them in the vehicle screaming at the same time. I didn't think I would ever hear the same again. Of course, I was yelling, "It's OK! It's OK!" over and over again. I finally pulled over on the gravel shoulder, stopped, and turned the engine off. They had stopped making all the noise by that time and started crawling up on the back seat again.

I had turned around and was half mad. I said, "You guys have seen cars meet on the roads before. Why in God's name would you act like that?"

Sara answered, "We have never seen one coming straight at us though." I noticed that her eyes got bigger, and she was looking over my shoulder to the front of the pickup. In fact, they all were.

I figured another car was coming, and turning back around had another surprise in store. There were little people all over my pickup—and I mean, all over my pickup. I might add, none of them looked happy, and they all had their little weapons in their hands. To make things worse, I didn't recognize any of them.

I said, "Jamie? I think I'm going to need some help here."

Jamie answered, "I think we are all going to need some help. These are not our clan; I think we got over the boundary."

I didn't know what to do, so I started to run my window down when Sara said, "Don't, Wayne. Just wait a minute or two. You might get a face full of pain if you don't." I immediately took my hand off the switch, and Jamie and Sara crawled up into the front seat. I couldn't see the kids anymore; I figured they had crawled under the back seat again. Sara got right up next to the windshield and squinted through the window. She said, "I've seen that lady before, the one in the back behind the men. She is a clan elder and a healer like I am."

Sara waved at her and grinned and told us all to smile and act like everything was OK. Ha, I did not feel like smiling at all. I mean, the kids were still under the back seat.

All of a sudden, the people outside all lowered their little weapons and started moving around, off of my pickup. I didn't see any of them laughing or smiling though.

I watched them all mill around the pickup and asked Sara, "Now what?"

She answered, "I don't know. Let's just sit here and see what they do."

Pretty soon, the woman Sara recognized waved at us to come out of the pickup. I thought, *Ha, absolutely no way am I getting out.* They would probably have just loved to use the big boy as a pincushion, and that was not going to happen. I told Sara and Jamie that if they wanted to get out, go ahead, but I was staying right there. Sara looked at me with a funny expression on her face. I just know she was thinking, *You chicken s——*, but she didn't say it. She did say, "OK, Jamie and I will get out and talk to them."

Jamie immediately faced her and said, "Nope, I'm staying in here with Wayne and the kids," who were now, I might add, standing up in the back seat again, looking out the window at all the other little people walking around the pickup.

Sara just snorted and said something under her breath. She looked at me and asked, "How do I open the door and get out?" I reached clear across the seat, in front of Sara and Jamie, and unlatched the passenger door. I had to kinda lie down a little to do that, and when I sat back up, all the little people outside had those little bows drawn again.

I asked Sara, "You sure you want to do this?"

She said, "Yes...what choice do I have? And if they try to get in here or try to hurt me, you are going to see something that is going to shock you a whole big bunch."

I looked at Jamie, and he winked at me and whispered, "She's mad now." I thought, *When this is all over, I have to find out about this.*

When Sara pulled the latch and started to crawl out, I heard someone say her name, but I couldn't see what was going on. She did close the door behind her though.

Jamie was standing above the passenger-side window, looking down and watching. I asked, "What's happening? Is Sara OK?"

He was kinda giggling and said, "Oh, yes, she is just fine." I did notice that most, or a lot, of little people were moving away from that side of the pickup and sort of looking back over their shoulders with expressions on their faces that are hard to describe.

She had been out there for some time, maybe five or six minutes, and I was just getting ready to get out myself when the door opened and Sara crawled back in. She started giving me directions where to drive to because that clan wanted to meet me.

I said "What?" I expressed my total concern about meeting any of them and then, trying a little humor, said, "If they break out a big cooking kettle and start looking at me and licking their lips, I'm running." Jamie just about fell out of the seat laughing. Sara didn't laugh, but she did smile, and said that I couldn't outrun them even if I wanted to. I said, "Thanks. That makes me feel real good." Then Sara did laugh.

I followed Sara's directions and ended up parking by a bridge over a creek that I did not know the name of. We all got out and I locked the vehicle, and then we followed Sara for about a quarter mile on a trail that paralleled the creek.

We came to another of those oak and fir thickets, and I had to get down on my knees and crawl for about fifty feet. We came out into a glade by the creek. My God, there were little people everywhere.

They had the same little houses or huts that Jamie's family had, but a lot more of them. Usually when I came into Jamie's family area, I was met with touching and laughing, but it wasn't like that here. In fact, most of the little people were still armed, and there were no children in sight; they must have all been in the houses. It gave me the creeps. They seemed kinda cordial to Jamie, Sara, and the kids, but not to me. At least they weren't looking at me and licking their lips. Heck, they weren't looking at me at all.

I didn't feel very wanted and told Jamie that I was going back to the pickup and would wait for them there. With that, I turned around and started back. Boy, I found out that wasn't the thing to do. All of a sudden, there were about a dozen little people blocking my way with their bows drawn and aimed right at me.

Sara came unglued. I don't think that is the right word, but I had never seen her that mad. I swear, the tree limbs were swaying, dust and leaves blowing everywhere, and a loud noise in the air like a tornado. At least that's the best way I can describe it. I don't know whether I fell down or was knocked down, but I ended up lying on the ground with my arms covering my head.

It only lasted about thirty seconds and then immediately stopped. I was rather hesitant to uncover my head and look up, and when I did, I must say I was shocked—or a little confused.

All the little people, except Jamie and his family, were sitting on the ground with their heads bowed and with their arms straight out and hands on the ground. There wasn't a weapon in sight.

Sara was standing directly in front of most of them and emitting a very fast chattering sound or vibration-like sound. I thought that she must be talking extremely fast in their language. I always knew they had a different language than mine; I think Jamie mentioned it a long time ago. Anyway, her hands were on her hips, and she looked totally pissed, for lack of a better word. She actually was glowing all over.

Jamie was off to the side with the kids, and when I looked over at him, he looked like he was grinning. I sure didn't feel like grinning.

I started to get up, and Sara looked at me, stopped chattering, and said, "Wayne, come here."

All I could think to say under the circumstances was, "Yes, ma'am." I continued to get up and went over to her.

I noticed that none of the little people on the ground were looking up at her, and some of them were actually shaking. I thought that they must be really scared. Not a little scared, but a big bunch scared.

Sara waited until I walked up to her and then told me to go back to my vehicle and wait for her and her family. She said that they would be coming shortly and then added that no one would bother me. And then she looked all around at the little people on the ground and made a chattering noise. I immediately got down on my knees and crawled out of there. After I got through the brush thicket, I felt like running, but I didn't.

I had been back to the pickup for about five minutes when they showed up. Jamie and Sara appeared to be arguing. Darcy was the first to get in; I had already opened the passenger door. She said, kinda under her breath, "I told you never to get my mother mad."

I said, "Wow, tell me about it." She wasn't laughing, but Davey giggled when he got in.

When Jamie and Sara got in, I found out what the argument was about. Sara had destroyed all the others' weapons, or at least all the ones that were out in the open and not in their huts. Jamie was upset about it because he didn't think they would be able to hunt for food without the weapons. Sara said she was sure they had more than enough weapons left in their huts.

Sara jumped up beside me in the seat while Jamie closed the door. She said, "I want to go home."

I said, "Me too."

On the way back, no one said a word.

Well, I made a comment. "My God, Sara, are you a goddess or a witch or something like that?" It was real quiet for a second, and then the whole family just about died laughing. In fact, I started laughing too. Sara said we would talk about it later. I got a feeling she wanted to tell me something that she didn't want the children to hear.

CHAPTER 22

The next day, as usual, I was working outside around the garden when I heard the familiar *pop* behind me. Not turning around because I was bent over with something in my hands, I heard Sara say, "It's just me, Wayne."

I stopped what I was doing, turned around, and said hi. At first she didn't say anything; she just looked at me without smiling. I did not have a good feeling in my stomach.

She finally said, "We have to have a talk. Let's go over to the steps and sit down. Linda isn't home, is she? I see her car is gone."

I told her that Linda wasn't working but had gone to town shopping and would probably be home in a couple of hours.

We went over to the back porch steps and sat down. She sat as far as she could away from me and just looked at me. Finally, she said, "Wayne, I'm going to tell you some things that I'm not supposed to. I know you already know things about us that no other big person knows, at least to my knowledge, but I'm going to tell you something about me and a little bit about our religion, which I know you are interested in. Now first, you know that I am a healer and a clan leader, but there is more."

I answered, "I figured that I was missing something after seeing what you did yesterday—or seeing what I think you did, anyway."

Sara said, "What I did yesterday was necessary for our safety. We all were in grave danger, not just of injury, but to our very existence. They were capable and had the intent to destroy all of us, including the children. To put a stop to it, I had to use certain powers that I have. Now that you have seen these powers, I am going to have to try and explain them, which is going to be quite difficult since you know very little about our religion and such.

"I want you to understand why they reacted the way they did yesterday. At first, they thought you had taken us against our will, and they were after you, but when I explained that we were with you intentionally, they were angry at us for being with you. You see, as you know, all clans have a strict doctrine against having contact with big people. They invited us to their camp for one reason: to kill us. I'm sure you noticed that no children were present. They didn't want their young people to see what they were going to do.

"The clan elders of this group do not have the powers that I do, or there would have been a tremendous battle. Something that I am sure glad didn't happen because we all would have suffered.

"OK, not only am I a healer and a clan elder, I am what you would call a priestess or a sorceress—or a mixture of both. Now let me explain. I know a little about your religion; it is very similar to ours. Let me explain the exceptions. First, you believe that your God is masculine. We believe our supreme being, or god, is feminine. I believe that your culture has come across this before because I'm sure you have seen or used the phrase 'Mother Nature.' That is almost the perfect description of our god.

"Now, we worship our god a little differently than you do yours. When you want to talk to your God, you pray. When our people want talk to our god, they come and see me—or, in other words, they talk to our god through me. I'm not saying that our people don't pray, but seldom do they get answered except through me. Not only do I carry the voice of our Mother, but she has given me powers such as you saw yesterday. There are other clan matrons that have the voice of Mother, but not many have the power given by Mother like I do. I did not ask for this power; it was given to me upon birth. Some of my people call me a witch; some call me a sorceress. In my clan, I am called a priestess, which is probably the most correct because I do not worship or do evil. I try to do the best I can for my people.

"Do you understand, Wayne?"

She had water in her eyes, and I thought she was going to cry. I reached over and grabbed her and gave her a big hug and kissed her on the forehead, something that I had never done before. Heck. I'd hardly ever touched a little person before, except Davey and Darcy when they were hurt. Little people were always touching me. Anyway, it kinda surprised her, and she jumped back with hands on her hips and a stern look on her face and then laughed and threw her arms around my neck and gave me a big hug.

She started to walk away but turned around, saying, "You know, you are a pretty good person for a big person," smiling and giving me a wink.

"Heck, I *have* to be nice to you," I answered. "I don't want you using any of those powers of yours on me," and laughed.

She just grinned great big and left with a pop.

I was left sitting on the steps, wondering what was in the future.

CHAPTER 23

I never saw Jamie or any of his family over the next few months. Linda and I were trying to find a place to move to, and I figured that Jamie was trying to do the same.

Linda and I had sold the property that we previously had up for sale, and I confronted the new owners of the property behind our house with the intent to try to buy some of it, but to no avail. They evaded me for some time, and when I finally contacted them, they said they didn't want to sell. So we went on with our plans to relocate.

We finally decided to move closer to some of our children and picked out a place near the coast, situated near one of the major rivers. We had enough money to secure the sale until we sold our house and refinanced the new home, which went through in about three months.

I lost contact with the little people until I went back to the old place; I had almost finished moving but had a few miscellaneous items and boxes left. I was by myself; Linda had already started to work again, doing the same thing, but, of course, at a different location.

I really missed Jamie and his family. I had always been accompanied by somebody while looking for a house and moving—usually Linda. I was sure that was why they never came to see me, and that's also the reason I couldn't try to find them. For some reason, they still wouldn't let Linda see them. I guess it was their strict privacy code, but I think it was more than that. The little people women just did not trust the females of our race, and I never was told the real reason for that. Of course, you know who had all the power in the little people families.

A couple of times, Linda almost bumped into some of them, and it really scared them, bad. I think all of Jamie's family had strict orders not let Linda see them. I remember when Davey and Jamie first made contact with me. They thought they were in a lot of trouble. Later, I heard about the clan council that was held, but I guess Sara went to bat for them, of course, and I don't think anyone in their right mind would go against Sara.

Anyway, I was sweeping out one of the shops when Davey popped up, literally. I laid down the broom I was using and gave him a big hug. I don't think he liked that; he got all red in the face.

Of course, the first thing he said was, "Where's Bruno?" I said that Bruno was at our other house where we were living now. He said, "Oh, I knew he was gone. I came over about every day when we were in this area to see him. I really miss him." God, I felt terrible. Here was this little maybe two-foot-tall boy, standing in front of me with tears running down his face, biting his cheeks trying to keep from crying. Good grief, what could I do?

I dropped down on one knee, held my arms out, and said, "Come here!"

He ran over to me and I gave him another big hug. Good Lord, I had tears in my eyes too.

I then felt other little arms on and around me, and of course, there were Jamie, Sara, and Betsy. No one said a word; they just held on to me. I then said something stupid like, "Wow, I think I was missed," or something. Sara hit me on the head and everybody started laughing. I said, "Well, I missed you guys," and got another hug.

I noticed that Darcy wasn't there. I asked where she was and got a funny look from everybody. I immediately thought of eagles and got a sick feeling in my stomach. They must have noticed the change in me, and Jamie said, "No, no, Wayne. She is all right, it's just that we have a problem. Let me try to explain...

"In our culture, we are not allowed to marry within the clan, of course, because most of them are family. I believe your culture is same in this respect. Anyway, when one of our young people feel that's it time to marry, usually around the age of seventeen or eighteen, he or she is allowed to visit other clans or families. Well, three of our young people, two girls and one boy, were allowed to visit a family across the river. Darcy was one of them. It was a family related to the clan we bumped into when we went for a ride in your vehicle.

"When the young people came home, having been gone for six days, Darcy was not with them. When questioned, the boy and girl said that a boy really liked Darcy. He was the son of a clan matron and not a nice person at all. He apparently told the boy and girl that Darcy wanted to stay with them and that they should go immediately. They never got to see Darcy before they left.

"The boy and girl had heard that the family had lost its head healer from old age and disease. They had heard of Sara and knew she was a healer. They understood that the family had hoped that Darcy might be a healer someday, like her mother. The family did not know that Sara was also a priestess with the power of Mother. For some reason, their relatives on this side of the river never told them about their experience with Sara, probably because they were ashamed of their intentions."

Sara gave me a strange look and said, "Darcy is my firstborn daughter. She not only inherited some of my healing powers, as the other family thinks, but she also has been blessed by Mother. Darcy is not aware of to what extent yet. She is aware of some power she has that other young people do not have, but she is still too young for the extensive training that is required."

She said that Darcy had been gone for more than two weeks and that she was getting a little worried. She thought that Darcy should be home by now. Sara was reluctant to intervene because she was afraid of what might happen. She knew Darcy was all right. If Darcy was under any emotional stress, Sara said that she would know it.

Jamie said, "Wayne, the bad thing about all this is, we don't live over in the woods anymore. The family has moved across the big river and is sharing an area with another small clan." He said it was a half a day's travel for them to get back here, and the only reason they happened to be here now was because of Darcy: they had received word from the other family that they would be in this area today. He said that they had been to their old campsite, but nobody was there yet.

I said, "Jamie, I don't particularly want to be here when you and Sara confront the other family. What do you expect them to do? What are you and Sara going to do?"

Jamie said, "Oh, we didn't expect you to be here. But you won't be involved anyway."

I said, "Oh, sure. Have you ever seen me not get involved? I'm probably going to get stuck full of little arrows and darts." I added, "Sara, I hope you brought along a lot of that gold wonder dust of yours."

She just grinned at me and said, "Don't worry, Wayne. I will take care of my big man friend," and then laughed. I did not laugh.

Jamie and his family left, and I went back to sweeping the shop. He said they would be back when it was all over and had Darcy with them. I told him that I wouldn't leave until then.

I finished with the shop and then loaded a bunch of boxes in the pickup. I was just getting ready to sit down on the steps when Davey showed up. He was pretty excited. He said the other family had showed up, a whole bunch of them, and they were not being nice to his mom and dad. I asked, "What do you mean, not nice?" And he said that there was a lot of yelling and screaming going on. I said something like, "Oh, damn," and asked him where Darcy was. Had he seen her? And he said no, but that they said they had brought her.

OK, I thought I would go over and make an appearance. Probably a dumb decision, but I had to do something. I told Davey to lead the way and took off.

We got halfway across the field, and I heard a bunch of chattering and noise off to my right in the trees. I turned to Davey and asked him what it was, and he told me it was some little people yelling. He then added that it sounded like Darcy. Davey and I immediately headed in that direction.

Coming around a big oak tree, we came upon three little people. One's hands were tied behind his or her back and was making an awful noise, meanwhile trying to kick the other two. The one with hands tied was Darcy. She didn't look too good. Darcy had a piece of gray duck tape hanging off of one cheek and blood on the other, and coming from her mouth. She was covered with dirt and leaves as if she had been rolling around on the ground. One of the other two was trying to hit her with a stick; the other had a bow with an arrow in place.

Everything happened real fast; Darcy saw us, her eyes got real big, and she stopped screaming. The one holding the bow and arrow started to aim it in our direction. I told Davey, who already had his bow and arrow in hand, to shoot that son of a bitch, which he did, and that I was running for Darcy.

Just before I got to Darcy, I took a right-hand swipe at the one with a stick, and to my disbelief, I actually hit him in the side of the face.

I grabbed Darcy under my left arm and ran like the dickens back to the field. Of course, Davey beat me back and was waiting for me. Davey was still red in the face and looked like one pissed-off twelve- or thirteen-year-old, little-person boy.

I sat down to take off the tape that was on Darcy's wrists. Meanwhile, Darcy was telling me that we were all in trouble now. She said that I had hit the clan matron's son and how much of a no-no that was, meanwhile thanking Davey and me for saving her—and after her hands were free, hugging us both, over and over and over again.

I heard a movement and turned to Davey. He had dropped his bow on the ground, looking past me with big eyes, and then got real close to me. I stood up and turned around. There were about fifteen or twenty little people, all armed, with their bows pulled back and aimed right at us.

I thought *They are going to shoot! They are actually going to shoot*. I told the kids to get out of there fast—"Real fast, like I know you can do."

Darcy said, "No! We're not going to leave you."

I answered, "Well, then, you'd better use some of the powers your mother said you inherited from her."

She hesitated and said, "I don't know how."

I then said, "Well, kids, you'd better call your mother, or we're in a lot of trouble." I'd hardly got that out of my mouth when I heard a loud screech. I said something like, "Oh, shit!" and grabbed and pulled both of them under me on the ground. I felt the pain as those damned little arrows started to hit me.

I found out later that those little arrows had poison on them, and apparently that's the reason I lost consciousness real fast. I thought I heard and felt something like a boom or crash, something real loud, just before everything went dark.

I woke up not really knowing where I was. Somebody must have rolled me over because I was on my back, looking up at the sun.

Sara was shaking me and trying to get me to sit up and drink something, which I did. It tasted terrible, and I almost threw it up, but she made me drink it all. I felt very dizzy and told her so. She said it would pass and made me lie back down.

I noticed that the rest of the family—Jamie, Darcy, and Davey—were standing around me. They were all touching me, and Darcy was crying, which kinda bothered me. I closed my eyes and apparently went back to sleep.

The next time I woke up, I was lying on my back in a small meadow surrounded by trees. My God, it was beautiful. The color of everything was real bright and vivid, and there was a sparkling mist in the air. I didn't recognize where I was and was kinda scared to find out.

I was covered with a blanket, or something like a blanket. It was real soft and real light. In fact, it seemed like it was floating and not really touching me.

I raised my head and looked around. Good grief, there were little people everywhere, and I mean everywhere. There must have been at least a hundred, probably more. They were standing around in groups, talking. I had never seen that many little people in one place together. They had on brightly colored clothes; it was all just beautiful. I thought, *Now, I suppose, I'm in little people heaven*, and then, *Oh, well, at least I don't feel any pain*. I'll take it.

One of them must have seen me move because all of a sudden, they were all around me, talking to me in my language. I heard a light noise like a squeal, and they started to move back.

Sara came through and knelt beside my head. She asked me how I felt. I answered, "Fine—I'm just a little light-headed and confused. My gosh, everything is so pretty. Where am I?"

She laughed and said, "You're not far from where you were. We just carried you into the woods, out of sight." She said that the reason that everything looked so pretty was because of the medicine she gave me. She added that it should wear off anytime now and that I had been asleep for about two hours.

I told Sara, "Thank you for arriving in time to save us."

Sara gave me a funny look and said, "Wayne, I didn't do anything. When Jamie and I arrived, it was all over. I guess you were already out from the poison that was on the tips of the arrows."

"OK, Sara, maybe you'd better tell me what happened."

Sara said that after I'd covered the children with my body, Darcy had screamed for help from Mother just as the arrows started to fly. Sara said that when she arrived, I had ten arrows in my back; neither Darcy nor Davey were hit, and all of the other clan's hunters were gone. Sara said that she thought Darcy had called for help from her because she had heard her scream, but Mother Above came to her aid.

Sara said that when Darcy was young and Sara knew that she had inherited the power of Mother, she had told her to ask for Mother's help in an emergency. "Darcy had apparently forgotten about that when the eagle got her, or you and she would never have had to suffer that ordeal. Darcy didn't forget this time."

Sara told me that I could try to stand up, and I did. I was still a little dizzy, but things were starting to look normal. I noticed all the little people move back, away from me.

I told Sara that I had to leave to get home before dark and that I would be back in two days for my last trip to clean up, if Jamie or she would be around.

Sara said that they would try to be there. They thought that they could stay with a neighboring family that they had ties with for a couple of days.

As I was getting ready to leave, I said, "Well, I hope Mother gave the clan that tried to hurt Darcy, Davey, and me a just punishment."

Sara looked at me for a minute and said, "Wayne... she took them away."

"I know that. But I hope she punishes them for kidnapping Darcy and trying to hurt us."

She said, "Wayne! They are gone *forever*—all the people that were involved."

I just looked at her for a minute before I left and thought, *Boy, that's quite a bit different than our society would have handled it, that's for sure.*

CHAPTER 24

I got to my pickup and actually felt pretty good, con-
sidering. I mean, after what I had just gone through,
I was lucky just to be walking. I had to get away from
all those little people. I don't think I was really thinking straight as it was, and I know how close to some of
them that I had been, almost like family, but wow, things
just kept happening when I was around them. I mean, I
couldn't imagine what I was in for next.

I felt under my tee shirt for damage to my back, but
when I got to the house and looked in the bathroom
mirror, I found no evidence of injury. My back did feel
hot, like maybe a sunburn felt, but that was all. Other
than that, I felt perfectly normal.

That's all right. I felt those damned little arrows go
into my back, and I didn't want a repeat performance,
that was for sure. Also, I had to throw the tee shirt away.
The holes were quite evident, and there was blood all

over it. It gave me the creeps when I took it off and looked at it. I had a sweatshirt in the pickup that I put on.

I still wondered what all those little people were doing there in the pretty place. Like I said before, I have never seen that many of them together at one time before. In fact, I didn't recognize any of them but Sara. I wondered where Jamie and the kids were at. I figured that I would find out in a couple of days.

It took about two hours to drive to our new home. Boy, when I got there, I was on a real high. I don't have any idea what Sara had given me, but I felt good. I mean, I didn't feel drugged. I just felt on top of the world. Wow, I liked it.

Linda was already home, and I just gave her all kinds of smooches. She said, "Boy, you are sure happy. You must have had a good day or something."

I said, "Oh, not really. I'm just happy to be home and with you," and gave her another big hug and smooch. She just laughed.

Two days later, I went back to the old place. I told Linda that I had forgotten to check the barn and had to sweep out the gear room. She wasn't working that day and almost came with me, but said she was going to stay and unpack. That was a relief because I didn't know what I was going to do if she decided to go.

Anyway, when I got there, I didn't see any little people around for about two hours. I was walking around the back corner of the barn and ran right into Jamie and darn near knocked him over. He just sputtered and stammered like all little people do when surprised. I laughed. He told me to be quiet and then started laughing with me.

He said, "I didn't know if you would get here. We've been over at the old campsite for quite a while."

"Jamie, Sara and I didn't set a time to meet. Besides, you people don't have clocks or watches, so it wouldn't do any good anyway."

He sputtered and stammered some more and said, "We don't need them. We use the sun." I just loved to get the best of Jamie. I had him, and he knew it. "Besides," he said, "I absolutely see no use in telling time like you people do."

I said "OK, OK, I understand. Where are Sara and the kids?"

"They're over at the old campsite. I was sent to find you."

We started to cross the field, and I got a funny feeling that something was up. I mean, Sara and the kids could have come to the house to see me.

We got to the campsite, and I was down on my hands and knees, crawling through the brush, when I heard a commotion and looked up. Good grief. All those little people that I had seen two days prior were there, I guess, and Jamie's family as well. Gracious! The forest was absolutely full of little people.

Of course, gobs of them, mostly Jamie's family, were surrounding me and trying to touch me, like they always do. It was cool, I have to admit. There were lots of tears and laughing.

Boy, I couldn't believe all the food that was there, mounds of it—and I mean mounds. Like I've said before, little people will use any excuse to party, and I was it on this day.

Little Betsy had been holding onto my right hand's little finger all this time. When things started to calm down a little, I could hear a little "Grandpa Wayne, Grandpa Wayne."

I swung around real quick and picked her up, holding her at arm's length up in the air and said, "Who is this beautiful girl?" She just squealed and giggled. Everybody else was laughing too. I then got a great big hug around the neck.

Darcy and Davey came up to me. I said, "Boy, you two look better than the last time I saw you."

Davey said, grinning, "Yah, you do too. You looked like a pin cushion and were sound asleep."

"You have a lot of humor for somebody your age. By the way, you had a bow...why didn't you protect us?"

He just stood there a second and then said, "I think I dropped it." Everybody started to laugh again.

Darcy said, "Wayne, I want to talk to you in private today before you leave."

I answered, "Sure, when things start to calm down a little."

And then here came John, Jamie's great-grandfather, with his usual cup of hooch. He didn't say a word, just held it out to me and grinned. Now that John, he is a good man, always ready to have a good time. I told John that was the only cup I could have because I had a long way to drive when I left. He looked a little disappointed. He probably wanted to carry me home again like he did that one time before with his friends.

I had been there for about a half hour; things were calming down when Sara came up to me. Actually she hadn't been very far away. Jamie and his family had been staying pretty close to me. Anyway, she said, "About the other day, when Jamie and I got there and it was all over and the only people there were you and the kids...both of them were holding on to you and crying." She said she had pulled the arrows out and put medicine on my back and then made me drink some stuff she had mixed. "That's all there was to it. Although, with that many poisoned arrows in you, if I had been too much later, you wouldn't be here today."

That brought up a point. I said, "Sara, I understand that when little people die, they turn to dust in a very short time. I was wondering. Since I've had so much of your medicine in me from the past, is that going to happen to me?" She laughed and said no, she didn't think so. She wasn't sure about my life-span though. She indicated that I might live a little longer than a normal big person. I had heard that before. She said a legend of theirs tells of this happening a long time ago, before her time.

I asked Sara if Darcy was going to get in trouble. She asked, "For what?"

"For making that whole bunch of hunters go away."

She stood there for a moment and then said "No. Mother did that, not Darcy. Besides, she was taken and held against her will. If it had been me, it would have been a lot worse."

I asked, "How could it be any worse? They're gone." Sara said that she would have made the whole tribe go away. "Good grief," I said. "Sara, you would have killed the whole tribe?" She said that the whole tribe knew of the kidnapping, not just those hunters and the matron's son.

She added, "Wayne, we do not say 'kill' or 'killed' when we talk of making another person cease to exist. We say we made them go away because if we die violently and not by natural causes or disease, we vanish or disappear immediately. Otherwise, it takes a day or two for our bodies to go away."

I just looked at her dumbfounded. She talked of taking somebody's life, or dying, so easily.

I asked her, "Sara, do you believe that when you die, your spirit goes somewhere or you have another life?"

"Of course. Mother takes us. I don't think it's a good thing, though, if she has to take us like those hunters. I don't think they're having a very good time, especially the matron's son."

I asked what would happen with the rest of the clan since so many hunters were gone. She said that they probably had enough hunters left, or they would be taken into another family that they were related to—more than likely the latter because most families are related one way or another.

Jamie was standing next to us and listening. He said that is what their family did. They had moved in with a small clan across the river that was related to them. In fact, almost all of that clan was here today with two other related clans from across the river. Most of them just wanted to see a big person up close. He said that he told them they weren't any different, just uglier. He and Sara thought that was real funny. I told him that he had better be quiet, or I would tell some stories about him.

He didn't laugh anymore, but a lot of other little people did.

I asked Jamie, "Where is your new home? You haven't told me yet." He looked at me, thinking. I asked, "Well, aren't you going to tell me?"

He said, "Yes, yes. I'm just trying to figure out how." He started by saying it was really a long ways from there, at least for them. "It takes a long time to get there, a full half of a day, and you know how fast we can travel sometimes. But that's the trouble. We can't travel fast most of the time because we have to cross two rivers, and gosh, I don't know how many of your roads, but a lot. We have to travel through two other clans' territories. By the way, those two clans are here today, they are all related."

I had a thought and interrupted Jamie. I asked, "What direction are you talking about?"

He pointed west, or almost west, and said "That way."

I said, "Jamie, there is a big city that way." He said that they kinda go around it.

I asked, "Do you go over any mountains?" He answered no big mountains, a hill or two. I said, "Jamie, that's the direction I moved, but farther and close to the ocean."

We just stood there and looked at each other a minute, and then Jamie motioned for Sara to come back over to us. He asked Sara, "Did you know Wayne and Linda moved in that direction?" pointing west again.

She said, "Yes; he doesn't have to travel far from our clan area to get to his new home."

Jamie got a little red in the face and asked, "When were you going to tell me and the kids?"

She said, "Now Jamie, don't get all in a tizzy and upset, for gosh sakes. I would have mentioned it sooner or later. It's just that I didn't really know where exactly that Wayne and Linda moved, only that they moved in that direction."

I think Jamie was a little put out, and I was wondering how Sara knew in what direction we had moved and Jamie didn't.

About that time, Darcy came up and grabbed my arm. She said, "Come with me. I want to show you something." She pulled me to the other side of the group of people and around behind a big tree and told me to kneel down, which I did.

She threw her arms around my neck and gave me a big hug, saying, "Thanks for saving me again. You and Davey are my heroes." I laughed and tried to make light of what she was saying before she started crying, which would probably cause me to get tears in my eyes. And then everyone would see it and start crying and try to hug me. There were already a heck of a lot of little people trying to watch us.

I stood up and said, "If I recall, it was you who really saved our bacon."

"Bacon?"

"Just an old expression. I mean you saved our lives."

"Oh...I may have, but I didn't know what I was doing. I was just yelling for help."

"Well, it helped, all right. It really helped. I wouldn't be here if you hadn't yelled. I don't know what they would have done to you and Davey. Boy, being friends with you and your family is really detrimental to my health and well-being."

"Just what does that mean?"

I could see she didn't take that right, so I added, "I'm just kidding, for gosh sakes, take a joke." I thought I'd take another stab at being humorous and said, "After all, if you weren't so darn pretty and cute, none of this would have happened. That young boy wouldn't have been so smitten over you."

Darcy stood up as straight and tall as she could and put both hands on her hips. She said, "Are you saying I caused all of this?"

Now I know little people do not understand some of our words and phrases, and in general, you have to be quite careful in what you say. Otherwise they end up getting their feelings hurt, and then look out—you know who's going to suffer in the end. In this case, I think what Darcy took offense to was the word "cute." Little people do not like to be called cute.

"No," I said, "I don't think you caused it. And by the way, when you and the other two young people went over to visit that clan, what made the clan matron's son so infatuated with you?"

She asked, "What does that mean?"

"Well," I said, "I understand that the boy wouldn't let you leave. He must have fallen in love with you, or something that would make him act that way." I asked, "Did you know him from before?" And she answered no. I asked, "Was he that way from the first, or did he get that way later, during your stay?"

She said "Later. After we had a few parties and stuff."

I just looked at her and asked, "Darcy, did you make out with that boy?"

She didn't answer at first, but then said, "A little."

"Darcy?"

She added, "Well, maybe a little more than a little. But I sure didn't say I would marry him or anything like that, and when he said that he was going to marry me, I said 'Absolutely no!'"

I said that apparently, he didn't like that answer.

She said, "That's when he went a little crazy and said that I could never leave his clan and if he couldn't have me, nobody could." She said, "Wayne, I know you couldn't hear him, but when they confronted us in the field, he told his buddies to kill us, all of us. And I'm sure they would have if Mother hadn't come to help. I screamed for help when I heard what he said."

I could see that she was getting ready to cry. She was looking down at the ground, not at me, and her little fists were clenched and hanging down at her side.

"Well," I said, "it's all over now, and we are all safe, that's the main thing. And by the way, I still think you are pretty and cute."

I was kneeling down when I said that, so I was looking directly at her. She looked me right in the eye and I could see that she gritted her teeth. Then she threw her head back laughed great big, jumped and threw her arms around my neck, and held on. I stood up and carried her around the tree.

Coming around the tree, it seemed like a thousand eyes were on me, I thought, *My God, did I do something wrong again?* then there was whooping and yelling and laughing and little people all over me, so I knew everything was all right.

Most of the little people there knew of the bond between me and Jamie's family, so I felt pretty good until Sara said "Boy, it's a good thing you are a big person, or I would do some worrying about this."

At that, I dropped Darcy, and she gave her mother a disgusted look and said, "Mother!"

I said, "Sara, I'm over three times her age and size, married, and her supposedly adopted grandfather—hmmm. I don't think so!"

I looked over at Jamie, who was rolling around on the ground laughing so hard he had tears all over his face. In fact, everyone thought it was a real joke—except maybe me and Darcy, who was still sitting on the ground where I'd dropped her.

CHAPTER 25

I got back to my new home just before dark. I had a difficult time getting away from all the little people. Of course, they wanted to continue to party, and I'm sure they did after I left. Jamie and I decided to meet back at the old place in two weeks. We didn't know where else to meet, being that neither of us knew where the other lived. Jamie promised to get better landmarks to his clan site for the next time.

When we did make contact two weeks later, he was extremely evasive on the camp area of his family. He said that the clan council that they had moved in with did not want him to meet with a big person, and all of his people living in the whole area were in a tizzy over it.

I didn't see anyone from his family around and asked him if he had come alone. He said that Davey had come with him, and that he was out hunting squirrels.

I asked him how he liked the new area where he lived. He said that it was OK, but he preferred the old one...he was still pretty upset with the new property owners. We both had noticed that they had started cutting trees and draining the wetlands. What I had predicted had already begun.

About that time, Davey showed up with a squirrel he had shot with his bow and arrow. He was beaming all over, one proud little boy. He said that he had been hunting this particular one for a long time, and he finally got it. He added that it was one smart squirrel, but he was smarter, and laughed.

I asked him if he was going to carry it all the way to his new home. He said, "Nope," that he was going to skin it, and his dad was going to cook it for their lunch. He looked at Jamie and said, "Huh, Dad?"

Jamie said sure, and that it was getting close to eating time anyway. He told Davey to go skin and clean the squirrel and that he would start a fire. He asked, "Hey, Wayne, have you ever eaten a squirrel?" I answered no. Jamie laughed and said, "Yes, you have, you just didn't know it."

I said, "Well, probably because I was drinking your grandpa's hooch while I was eating it," and we both laughed.

Jamie got his fire going, behind my old barn and started cooking their lunch. We sat around and talked about our past experiences. When the squirrel was done, he offered me a leg. I wasn't real sure about it, but I took it anyway. I was very surprised; it was delicious. It tasted something like chicken.

Listening to Jamie talk while he was cooking and while we ate, I started to really feel sorry for him and his family. Moving, for them, was a very traumatic experience. I mean, Linda and I had moved about every four or five years. It really meant nothing to us to relocate, but it wasn't the same for them. Jamie, his kids, parents, and grandparents had been born at the old site. Good grief. Jamie was almost in tears talking about it, and now they were not getting along with the clan they had moved in with.

I began to feel a little responsible. I don't know what more I could have done about them moving. I had tried to buy the property where their old campsite was.

I didn't want to tell Jamie, but we didn't particularly like where we had moved either, for a lot of reasons; the water tasted terrible and smelled worse. We didn't get along real well with the neighbors, who I didn't want to think about, let alone tell anyone about. Besides, if I'd told Jamie, he would undoubtedly have wanted to do something about it, and that's all I needed. Our new place was next to a river, and people walked all over our place without asking permission. It's rather awakening to get up in the morning, open the window blinds, and see there's someone standing on the river bank, looking at you. And our dogs, as I've mentioned, are outdoor dogs, so of course, they were barking all the time at fishermen, which didn't help matters.

Anyway, Jamie could not bring it upon himself to tell me where they lived, so I started to question him. I asked if it was near the highway that runs from the big city to the coast. He looked away and, kind of under his breath, said yes.

I asked, "Did it take long to get to that highway from your camp?" He said no, that the highway runs through their hunting area. A light bulb went off in my head. I asked, "Hey, Davey, do you like eating birds better that eating squirrels?"

He answered, "Not really. And those geese are big and mean unless you hit them just right with an arrow." Davey then just looked back and forth between me and his dad. He asked, "Dad, did I say something wrong?"

Jamie just looked down and said, "No, son, it's all right. Wayne had a good idea where we lived, or he wouldn't have asked you that question. And I would have told Wayne where we lived anyway, no matter what the elders said. Besides, your mother told me to tell him and that she would take care of it if something came up."

I thought, *I wouldn't cross Sara for anything.* Those little people of the other clan probably didn't know Sara like I did. *Lord, I've seen what she can do.* I looked at Jamie and said, "You live in or around that big bird refuge, don't you?"

He answered, "Yes, but not really in it. Up on one of the hills covered with oak trees, behind it."

I said, "I know exactly where you mean. In fact, I have a good idea—why don't you and Davey ride back with me, and I will drop you off real close to your home."

Jamie turned kinda white and asked, "In your pickup?"

"Sure, why not? I can get you and Davey home faster than you can because of all the rivers and roads you have to cross." I added that they would have to hide on the floor going through the towns and in places people might see them.

Davey, a typical teenager, said, "Yah, Dad, let's do it, that would be fun."

Jamie, on the other hand, wasn't at all sure. I think he was remembering his last experience in my vehicle.

Davey and I were both standing there, looking at Jamie. He was looking down at the ground, clearing his throat. I was laughing like mad inside, but I didn't dare show it.

Finally, he said, "Oh, all right. But if I think Davey and I should get out, you promise to let us out."

I grinned and said, "Jamie, do you think I would keep you in the pickup if you didn't want to be there?"

He said, "You bet, you would." He wasn't smiling or laughing either.

We hung around the old place a little while longer; I was just checking things out. I wanted to make sure the hot water heater was turned off, and I made sure Jamie's cooking fire was totally out. The squirrel was all gone.

I opened the passenger door of the pickup, folded the seat forward, and told them to hop in the back seat. Davey jumped right in and crawled up into the seat. Jamie just stood there for a second and then slowly followed Davey. When he got up on the seat, he turned around and gave me a weird look: something between fright and anger. I don't think he would have agreed to come except for Davey. I told them they could sit or stand on the seat, but if I told them to, they had to get on the floor and cover up with the blanket that was there. They both agreed.

After I closed the gates, we were on our way. I could see Davey in the rearview mirror, but I couldn't see Jamie. I asked Davey where his dad was, and he said he was on the floor. I stopped the vehicle, looked over the seat at Jamie, and asked, "Are you going to ride down there all the way?" He answered no, that he was just getting adjusted, and got back up on the seat. I laughed and took off again.

Everything went just fine until we left the city, headed for the coast. It's a four-lane highway, so vehicles were going around us, and of course I was going slow because of my passengers. One car with four elderly women in it started to go around us, and just at that time, Jamie and Davey were both on that side looking out the window at the cars going by.

Well, I just happened to look to my left because the passing vehicle wasn't moving forward anymore but just staying with us. Now let me tell you, all I could see were large, round eyes and big, open mouths, and I thought I could hear some screaming. But probably that was my imagination...because it looked like they were all screaming. Anyway, I pulled over real fast and told Jamie and Davey to get on the floor. The other vehicle kept moving forward, weaving all over the highway.

I turned off of the highway onto a side road. I knew if I stayed on the side road, I would eventually come to the area I wanted to reach to let Jamie and Davey off. It took a lot of weaving in and out of different back roads, but I finally got to the area I wanted. I asked Jamie if he recognized any of the country we were in, and he said yes.

I went another couple of miles and pulled into a visitor's parking area for the refuge. No other cars were present, so I stopped and turned off the engine. I asked Jamie if he knew where we were at, and he answered yes again. I turned around in the seat, and Jamie was still on the floor. I asked, "Have you been down there the whole time? Well, probably, most of the time." Davey was standing in the seat.

He said, "I know where we are at, Wayne. Our camp is just over that big hill."

I could see no cars or people coming, so I got out and moved my seat forward so they could get out—which Jamie did immediately, with Davey following. I told them that if we saw or heard a car coming, they should leave fast like I knew they could. Davey said they would, but that they had to be real careful because they didn't know the area very well yet.

I asked if it wasn't more dangerous living so close to the refuge because there had to be more eagles around than where they from. Both of them immediately looked up into the sky. Jamie said that the eagles didn't seem to bother the little people so much in the new area because there were a lot more birds and small animals for them to catch and eat. He added that there were more big birds though, of all kinds.

There was a trail leading up a hill from the parking lot. I asked Jamie if he had been to the top where a viewing area was. He said of course, since they lived over the other side of that hill. I told him that I would come back to the parking lot in twenty-one days and meet him in the afternoon at the viewing area. I added if there were other people present, I would just hang around until they left. He agreed.

They both vanished with a pop, as little people do. I jumped. It seemed I'd never get used to it. Anyway, I got back in my pickup and left, driving out the gravel road to the main highway, which wasn't very far, and headed home.

There was a lot of traffic on the highway, and I met a state police car in about four miles. He immediately turned around behind me and turned on his overhead lights. It surprised me. I couldn't figure out what I had done wrong. After I pulled over and we both stopped, he walked up to my vehicle with his hand on his revolver, trying to see into my back seat.

I had my window open, and he told me to get out and to keep my hands in sight, which I did. He then looked all over inside my pickup. I asked what the problem was, and he seemed to relax—and, I might add, I did the same. He said that he had had a report of a vehicle like mine that was observed driving on this highway with two small children in the back, screaming for help. I told him that I hadn't noticed any other vehicles like mine on the road, but there had been a lot of traffic. He told me that he was sorry to bother me and left.

I got back in my pickup and just sat there, wondering what I would have done if Jamie and Davey had still been in the pickup. Good Lord! That could have been a real mess. I really didn't know how I would have explained it.

CHAPTER 26

Twenty-one days later, I drove back to the refuge parking lot and walked up the trail to the viewing area. I waited and walked around all afternoon, but Jamie didn't show. That really surprised me because Jamie usually always did what I asked him to do. In fact, I was worried that something bad had happened.

When I walked back to my pickup, I found a large feather stuck under my windshield wiper blade. I knew somebody had to have put it there. There was no other way it could have gotten there. I figured that some little person had jumped up on my hood and left it on purpose to let me know he or she had been there but didn't want to make contact with me. Now I really knew something was up.

I also had the strangest feeling I was being watched. There were no cars or big people in the parking lot, so it had to be little people or some animal. I looked all around but couldn't see anybody or anything suspicious.

I yelled, "You might as well come out and talk to me. I know you are out there watching me." I waited and waited, but nothing happened. Finally I said that I was leaving and would come back in two weeks, fourteen days. I would come at the same time of day, in the afternoon. I waited a little while longer and then left.

I wondered what was wrong. Probably something to do with the clan that they had moved in with. I had already been told that this clan didn't want anything to do with big people like me. There was nothing I could do but keep coming back to the parking lot.

I went back two times after that, with the same results: a feather under my windshield wiper blade, but no contact with anyone. I didn't know if I could leave a written note because I didn't know if they could read my written language. I had never discussed that point with any of them.

On the third time that I went to the parking lot, just before I left my vehicle, I left a note under my wiper that read: *What is going on? I am not going to keep coming back here for a feather.* Then I went and hid behind a bush instead of walking on the trail up to the viewing area. I waited for quite a while before anything happened.

Two vehicles drove into the lot and left, and then after about another half hour, I saw a blur or a little whirlwind come across the graveled lot and stop in front of my pickup. A person jumped up on my hood and looked at the note for a second before grabbing it and leaving the feather. I recognized him immediately. It was Davey.

I stood up and yelled, "Davey! You get over here right now!" The little whirlwind took off across the lot and then circled and came back in my direction and stopped right in front of me.

Davey just stood there and looked sheepish. He said, "Wayne, if I get caught doing this by anyone in the clan, I am in big trouble."

I answered that I didn't much give a damn. "And what would they do anyhow, kick you out? And if they did that, you could just come and live with me."

He looked up at me with a shocked look and his mouth hanging open, and then said "Really?"

I answered, "Of course. Anyone in your family is always welcome. You would probably have to let Linda finally see you."

Davey said, "I don't know if I could live in a big-person house. It's like living in a cave with a door on it. The ceiling is so high, and I would always be afraid of getting shut in."

I told him that he would get used to it, and that in any case, he could make a home on some property that I owned and nobody would bother him. All Davey could say was, wow, that would be cool. I asked him if his mom and dad knew he was coming to the parking lot. He said yes, but that they couldn't come because they were always being watched by the other clan's council members. I told him that I couldn't understand why his mother would be afraid of anybody, with her powers and all.

Davey said, "Wayne, the other clan's matron is just as powerful, and she said that the Mother Above told her that their people were not to come in contact with the big people."

I told him that I thought that was not true because the Mother Above saved my life and took away the little people that tried to kill me. I said, "Don't you remember? you were there."

He replied that he wasn't sure that she took away their lives to save me, but to save him and his sister. He said, "Remember, they said to kill all of us, and Darcy is the one that called for help from Mother." He was right, of course. That is what Darcy told me she heard the matron's son say: to kill all of us.

I stood there a minute and tried to think of what to say next. I really did not believe that the Mother Above would not help Sara and Sara's clan in a situation like this. After all, she could have stopped my contact with them a long time ago. Maybe she blamed me, somehow, for Sara's clan losing their heritage living area and territory.

I told Davey that I had to talk to his mother or father. He said that they wouldn't come, that they were afraid of what the other clan matron would do to the members of his clan. I said, "All right, I want to talk to the other clan's matron."

Davey just turned pale. He said, "Oh, come on, Wayne. She will hurt you bad—or worse."

"I don't think so. It sounds like she is just a bully. I think she needs to talk to a big person face-to-face."

Davey just stood there and looked at me and shook his head. He mumbled something like, "How did I get myself into this?" as he turned to leave. But then he said,

"All right...I'll tell mom and dad what you said," and was gone with a pop.

I didn't have time to tell him to come back in two weeks and let me know.

I did come back, every two weeks for two months. No one showed, not even a feather under my wiper blade. I felt a little sad and rejected, but there were apparently things going on that were out of my control.

I knew that Jamie and Sara were not going to let me talk to the other matron; they were probably thinking of my safety and were probably right. If she got really mad at me, there was nothing I could do to combat her, and I could imagine what she would do to me.

I really liked Jamie and Sara's family and clan, but I had already come to the conclusion that other clans of little people were not as nice or good to be around. In fact, some of them appeared to be really warlike. Little people are very smart and very sneaky. There is no doubt that some big people have suffered extremely in the past from some evil and mad little people.

I got real busy and couldn't keep trying to make contact with the little people, but they were always on my mind. In fact, I really missed them; after all, they had become like family to me. We were still having problems at our new house; the weather was rotten, and we were not happy living on the coast again. Finally we decided enough was enough and put our house up for sale.

When we sold our old house, it took about three months, so we figured it would take longer with the house on the coast since it was winter and the housing market was getting worse. Actually, it took about five months. One day, a family came to see our place and wanted to move in in a month. Wow. We had to find another place to purchase and move into fast.

We started to look just over the mountains from where we lived—actually, in the same area that Jamie and his family were supposed to be living. We looked for a week, in three separate towns and in the country—anything that was in our price range. We found nothing we liked.

Finally, after about two weeks of looking, we found what we wanted. I was sick with the flu, and Linda was driving. We had been seeing houses all morning when a real estate agent we had contacted earlier called us on my cell phone and told us about a house and twenty-two acres that had just come on the market. She was headed that direction and told us to meet her there.

Come to find out, Linda and I were only about two miles from there. When we finally found the address, I just about passed out. My God, the house and property was just on the other side of the bird refuges where Jamie and his family lived. In fact, you could see the hills where Davey said they lived from the house.

We both liked the property and house. There was a lot of work to be done, but we knew we could do it, and best of all was the fact that we could afford it.

To make a long story short, we made an offer, they took it, and we started moving in two weeks. I got over the flu just in time to start moving again. Needless to say, I was getting rather tired of moving, but we were sure glad to be leaving the coast place.

I was just wondering what Jamie, Sara, and the family were going to say when they found out where we lived. I knew one thing for sure: Davey couldn't stay away from Bruno, so I knew I was going to see him again.

I didn't know how to contact them to share the news anyway, but I figured they would find out, being that we were so close by.

CHAPTER 27

We had been living in our new place for about a month, both working hard to clean it up and trying to put things in place. We had to build the doghouses in a spot out of the wind and weather.

I hadn't tried to contact Jamie for over a year. I didn't know how to attempt it. I kinda figured that Jamie or his family would bump into me sooner or later at our new house. I just knew that our place had to be within their hunting boundaries or the new clan's territory. I was always watching for evidence of the little people being around me, like things I couldn't explain. Actually, like the things that happened before my first encounter with them. I really didn't notice anything unusual at first.

I have always liked to hunt for ducks and geese ever since I was a small boy, when my dad used to take me to my uncle's who had a duck-hunting pond. I had never been very successful since then; in fact, I had only killed two geese in my life until we moved to our new place near the refuge.

Approximately two months after we moved, the goose season opened in our area. I went and bought all of my licenses and permits (and believe me, there are more than a few) and decided to see if I could hit a goose on the opening day. I had been watching them fly over our property since we had been there, so I knew where to go and sit. In fact, it was in a bunch of blackberry vines on a small hill. Hopefully the geese would fly low enough over me, I thought, and just maybe I could hit one with my shotgun. I figured I could hide myself and the dogs, Mercy and Bruno, in the vines well enough.

Anyway, the dogs and I were out there, all set, and it was legal time to shoot. And here they came, probably a thousand geese, all spread out for about a mile. Boy, was I nervous and excited—probably more than the dogs who were sitting at my feet.

The geese were really loud and noisy, which just made it worse and more exciting. My God, I remember that I was so upset, and there were so many geese above me that I didn't know which one to shoot at. I finally picked out one, aimed my shotgun, and pulled the trigger. It just kept on flying away. I couldn't believe that I had missed; it wasn't that far. I was so shocked that I didn't shoot again, and all the geese left.

I looked down at Bruno, and he was just sitting there giving me a funny look, which I don't intend to try and describe. He finally got up, walked around the blackberry vines out of sight for only a couple of seconds, and returned with a dead field mouse. Dropping it at my feet, he then sat down and looked at me with kind of a grin on his hairy face.

I said something like, "I'll be damned," and thought I heard a small, high giggle come from behind the vines. Now, most people couldn't tell the noise was a giggle, but I could. I had heard it many times before, coming from little people. I ran around Bruno and the vines, but there was nothing there. I yelled something like, "I heard you!"

Needless to say, I went back to the house, deciding that my goose-hunting excursion was over for the day. I told Linda what had happened, leaving out the giggle, and she thought that it was extremely humorous. I don't think I should have told her. At least not the same day. I didn't feel too good about it.

Through the following year, I knew the little people were around me. I didn't know which ones, but I knew they were there. They weren't very secretive about it like they were before I first met them, but they still wouldn't show themselves. I wasn't upset about it. I figured they had their reasons.

I kept hunting geese during the seasons and finally started to hit a few of them. I kept losing them though. If I wounded a goose and it fell down out of sight, when I finally got there with the dogs, it was usually gone. Now, I have seen how fast they run, so at first I figured they just ran away when they hit the ground. Also, sometimes Bruno and Mercy would get to it before me, off in the brush somewhere, but before I got to it, they would come back to me acting really strange, and I couldn't get them to look for it again.

Now, I knew if a coyote or another dog had got there first, Bruno would have been right after them. Also, if it had been an eagle or any other big bird, I would have seen it fly off. No, it had to be little people for Bruno and Mercy to act the way they did. Oh, well, I didn't particularly like the taste of goose anyway. I didn't mind feeding a few little people.

I found evidence of little people in my garden the first summer. I had grown a few watermelons, and one morning after they were ripe, I found where someone or something had eaten about half of a big one and apparently had taken the other half with them. They had made a mess of the half they left, trying to make it look like an animal had done it, but I could tell the dried vine that had gone to the watermelon had been cut with a sharp knife, not chewed off like it would be by an animal.

Also, there were some ears of corn gone that I knew I hadn't picked, and some underground plants like potatoes and radishes gone. They always tried to conceal what they did, but I was in the garden every day and knew exactly what I had growing and where.

We have a large pond in our lower field. It's about an acre, and I have bass, bluegill, and some catfish in it. I don't fish in it too much, but the grandsons do, now and then. I'll see blue herons and other big birds, including eagles, get a fish or two. I knew the little people had been fishing in the pond. I found little pieces of worm and other stuff lying around on the ground and the dock.

One evening in the summer, I was watching the pond from the house, trying to catch sight of nutria that had just moved in about a week earlier. Now, I don't like nutria; they are rodents that are not native to our country, and they are vicious and nasty and look like big rats. They also make a mess of ponds.

Anyway, it was pretty dark, and I spotted the critter across the pond in the water next to the bank. I went and got my .22 rifle and stuck it out our family room window. I could hardly see it, but when it finally moved, I shot. Of course, I missed it; it was just too far away.

Just below and on the house side of the pond is our dock. It can't be seen from the house because of all the blackberry vines that grow there. When I shot at the nutria, there had been something on the dock because there was a big commotion, and I could see little waves in the water coming out from where the dock is. I got a big flashlight and the dogs, and I went down to investigate.

There was no animal on the dock when I got there, and I almost left—when I noticed a small stick lying on the edge. I bent down to pick it up and saw that it was a little homemade fishing pole, and the line was still in the water. It was just a little stick with real fishing line, not string, and it had a hook with some kind of bug on it. It was very primitive, not like Jamie's fishing pole, the one I had seen him use before.

I laid the little pole back down and then just laughed out loud. I must have scared that little person half to death when I shot my rifle. I said out loud, "I sure hate poachers, no matter what the size and who they are."

I then called the dogs and headed back to the house, thinking, *That was not a very smart thing to do. I might just suffer for that comment.* No, heck—I knew I was going to regret it. Oh, well, it was too late. I had already done it.

CHAPTER 28

One morning during the second summer that we lived in our present house, I took Mercy and Bruno for a walk like I usually did. We didn't walk on the road anymore, we walked on the property. It was hilly and brushy, and we had walking trails around and through it. The dogs got plenty of exercise, and I didn't have to worry about the cars on the road anymore. Anyway, I noticed Mercy was acting rather strange that morning, but she seemed OK, so I didn't think much about it.

At about nine o'clock, I decided to go to town and get a haircut. When I left, I noticed that Mercy was lying on the lawn by the deck and Bruno was in his doghouse. Nothing seemed amiss.

When I returned, driving down the driveway, I saw Mercy lying in the same place, but I didn't see Bruno. Mercy never moved while I parked the pickup, and that was unusual. I got out and walked over to her, and she still didn't move. I noticed a fly on her nose. Then I knew something was wrong for sure.

She had apparently died while I was gone. Her heart must have just stopped because I found no signs of trauma at all. She must have lain right there and died in her sleep. We knew that she had a large tumor on her stomach and that she was not near as active as she used to be, but we had no idea that she was that bad. Also, we knew that she was getting pretty old too, but we were not ready to lose her. We didn't raise Mercy from a pup like we did Bruno, but she was still one of the family.

Needless to say, I don't take things like this too good. I get pretty close with all of my animals. I immediately went into the house and called Linda at work and told her what had happened. I couldn't do a real good job of talking about it.

A couple of hours later, when I was able to do it, I got Mercy into my front-end loader tractor and headed down to the far corner of our property. She had loved running around on the property, and I figured that I would make sure that she stayed there forever.

Now let me tell you, this was not an easy thing for me, and it still bothers me to talk about it, but I knew it was something that I had to do.

The place I picked out was totally out of sight of our neighbors—or anyone, as far as that goes. I dug a large, deep hole and laid Mercy in it, and then Bruno came up and sniffed Mercy's nose. He knew something was wrong. His ears and tail were down and he acted strange. I don't know really how to describe it. Anyway,

I covered her up and then turned the tractor off and just stood there with Bruno.

It had been a couple of minutes when I felt something grab the little finger of my left hand. Looking down, I saw the cutest little face looking up at me. It was little Betsy. She said, "Grandpa Wayne," and was holding onto my finger with tears running down her face, just like me.

I started hearing all kinds of pops and commotion. And, looking around, I was surrounded by a lot of little people. Most of them I recognized from Jamie's clan. Jamie was beside Betsy on my left, and Sara with Darcy was on my right, holding onto my hand. Davey had his arms around Bruno's neck. All the rest were around me and Mercy's grave.

The little people around the grave all knelt down and placed their hands on the dirt, and then all of them started to make a whistling sound—something like singing, but in their own language. My God, it was kind of strange, but just beautiful.

Remember how I've always said how emotional the little people were, well, everyone there was crying.

After about ten minutes, everything went quiet, and Sara let go of my hand and stepped in front of me. She started talking in their language and then said in English, "Mother gives life and then takes life back. Mercy is with Mother now and always will be."

Now, I have always thought I was a pretty strong individual but you sure couldn't tell it then. I don't know whether it was Mercy's death or seeing all the little people after about three years, but I sure wasn't acting very cool and collected at the time. Finally, all of them led me over to a flat, grassy spot behind the tractor, and I have never been hugged or smooched on so much in my life. I think my emotions switched from grief and elation to total embarrassment. I know I turned beet red, I think from being squeezed so hard. Don't think for one minute that little people aren't strong because they are.

They were all telling me how much they had missed me and apologized for not coming to see me before. They were all trying to talk to me at once, and I was having a hard time understanding them. Finally, Jamie told them all to be quiet, and they started unpacking little baskets of food—a lot of food.

Grandpa John handed me a cup of hooch, and we both started laughing. My God, how I had missed these little people.

Jamie said that we had to talk; he had to catch me up on a lot of things. He saw Darcy coming and said, "Here comes one of those things," with a smile on his face.

Darcy walked right up to me. I was sitting down. She said, "Well, did you miss me, big guy?"

I answered, "Not really." That made Jamie and the others that heard my reply laugh.

She grinned and said, "I want you to meet somebody," and pulled a young man around from behind her. She said, "Wayne, this is Tim, my husband!"

I laughed out loud and said, "Howdy, Tim. I'm really glad to meet you." I added, "You married one of the most beautiful and intelligent young women that I've ever known in my life," and then I said, "you poor, poor boy."

Darcy squinted her eyes and pointed her finger at me, and the crowd just roared. She then laughed great big and threw her arms around my neck.

When she hugged me, I could feel her little, round tummy. I laughed, holding her back by the shoulders and said, "My God, girl, you are with child." Darcy turned beet red. Tim was already red, and the crowd was rolling on the ground now.

Jamie said, "Yup, I'm going to be a grandpa." He said that very loud and was beaming all over, I might add.

I noticed John standing close and grinning. I asked, "How many greats does that make you?"

He quit grinning and looked deep in thought and said, "I don't really know...four, I think."

I said, "Good grief."

Davey, who had been with Bruno all this time, walked over and said, "Wayne, I got a girlfriend, I think."

I laughed and asked, "What do you mean, think?"

He answered, "Well, I did this morning, but I'm not so sure now. Dad will explain." He then leaned into my ear, saying, "I'm thinking about coming and living with you."

Jamie heard him and added, "That's what he thinks. And Wayne, why did you say that to him?"

I answered, "I was serious. You or any of your family are welcome to come and live with me and Linda." He just looked at me, but I could see he was in thought. While all this was going on, little Betsy was still sitting on my knee like she always used to, although she was a little bigger now. I asked her, "I suppose you have a boyfriend too?"

She gave me a disgusted look and said, "Oh, really, I'm not that old, Grandpa Wayne. And Mama said I had to be at least fourteen years old."

I said, "You have to be older than that," and gave her a wink and a hug.

She giggled like little girls do and said, "All right, you can be my boyfriend."

I said, "All right, but remember, I'm your grandpa too." She had to think about that.

Sara came up to me then; she had been helping dish up food. She handed me a drumstick of some kind of bird, probably a goose, and asked, "Do you have time for me now?"

I replied, "Sure, why?"

She said, "Follow me," and then turned to Jamie and said, "you can come if you want. You know what I am going to tell him." He said no, that he was going to stay and eat.

We went around behind a big blackberry bush and she said, "OK, this is good enough. Take off your clothes."

I said, "What?" with a surprised look on my face.

She just grinned and said, "All right, just take off your shirt." She explained that they had been told that three years ago, when I had got mixed up with Darcy's so-called suitors, they had used a different, long-lasting poison on their arrows. She added that it could still be in my body and that she had to look at the scars, if there were any. Well, I knew there were some small, hard scars that sometimes itched, and I told her so as she looked at my back.

She took out a little container and put something on my back exactly where it itched. She gave me a little leather pouch and told me to go home and put the contents into a glass of water and drink it—and not to get too far away from a toilet. She grinned.

I asked her if I really needed the medicine or if she was just getting even with me for some reason. She looked dead serious at that and said, "You do it, or I may be talking over *your* grave, and I do not want to do that. If that happens, I will go back and make all of that clan go away." The look on her face scared the hell out of me. I decided to do exactly as she said. As she started to leave, she turned back and said, "Wayne, I'm really happy to see you. I've missed you." She asked how Linda was, and I told her fine. We walked back to the group.

Before we got there, Jamie ran up and said, "My turn," grabbed my hand, and turned me around. He said that he was sorry that he had not made contact with me earlier. He said that he had known we had moved to this place not long after we got here, but the trouble his clan was having with the other clan prevented it.

I asked him what had finally happened. How come they were here today? He said that Sara and the other clan matron had had it out and the Mother Above got involved. "Mother Above instructed the families to split the clan territory in half and to settle our differences, or she was going to settle matters in a different way. Apparently, the other clan matron didn't want to find out what the different way was, so she agreed." Now, according to Jamie, they had control of the west side of the territory, which included where Linda and I lived.

I told Jamie I thought that was cool and that I was glad it had all worked out finally. I then asked Jamie what Davey meant about he might or might not have a girlfriend and that he would explain. Jamie said that Davey's so-called girlfriend was the other clan's matron's daughter, and that it was just an arranged kind of a thing for trying to keep peace before the split in territory. He also said that Davey thought a lot more of the girl than she thought of him, and that she had a lot of boys after her. I told Jamie that I felt bad for Davey.

I asked Jamie how he liked hunting and eating geese, with a grin on my face. The question kinda caught him off guard, but then he laughed and said that I had better ask Davey—that he had been around me, Bruno, and Mercy almost every time that we were hunting. He then added that he thought that I had a better garden here than at the other place and then started laughing like that was the funniest joke in the world.

We went back to the group, and I ate and polished off a couple cups of John's hooch. Needless to say, I felt better going back to the house than I had leaving. I still felt real bad about Mercy, but I knew that time would heal, or at least make it not so bad.

I was sure glad that I had contact with the little people again; I had really missed them, as I said before. Riding the tractor back to the house, I remembered all my experiences with the little people in the past and also wondered what was in store for me in the future.

Made in the USA
Columbia, SC
09 November 2024

45810933R00124